MY BROTHER'S BRIDE

MY BROTHER'S BRIDE

RACHAEL ANDERSON

HEA Publishing

FOR MY FAVORITE KIDDOS,

BRIGHTON, KENNEDY,

DEVON, & TAYCEE

LOVE YOU!

OTHER BOOKS BY RACHAEL ANDERSON

Regency Novels
My Sister's Intended (Serendipity 1)
The Fall of Lord Drayson (Tanglewood 1)
The Rise of Miss Notley (Tanglewood 2)
The Pursuit of Lady Harriett (Tanglewood 3)

Contemporary Novels
Prejudice Meets Pride (Meet Your Match 1)
Rough Around the Edges Meets Refined (Meet Your Match 2)
Stick in the Mud Meets Spontaneity (Meet Your Match 3)
Not Always Happenstance (Power of the Matchmaker)
The Reluctant Bachelorette
Working it Out
Minor Adjustments
Luck of the Draw
Divinely Designed

Novellas
Righting a Wrong
Twist of Fate
The Meltdown Match

ONE

MUSIC PERVADED THE crowded ballroom, carrying couples through the steps of the quadrille, while onlookers clustered around the dancers, talking, laughing, sipping drinks, and observing.

Morgan Campbell, the Marquess of Brigston, did only the latter. He lingered near a door that opened onto a small balcony, where, every now and again, he'd feel a slight draft. Although it provided some relief from the heat in the room, the open door offered no other boon. This was not the country, and London air could never be described as fresh, not even on Grosvenor Street. Too many horses pranced about, too many bodies filled the streets, and too many unpleasant scents lingered as a result.

Only one month more and Morgan could leave his parliamentary duties behind and return to his coastal hometown of Cawley, Hampshire. Most considered the country to be a bore, but Morgan thrived there. The chirping birds, the salty breezes, the peace he felt every time he walked outside—Oakley Grange revitalized him as nowhere else could. It was London that tired him, or at least the endless social obligations. He despised frivolous chatter. It rang in his ears and made his head ache.

A servant offered Morgan a drink, but he declined, directing his attention towards the middle of the ballroom, where his younger brother, Jasper, danced with a paragon of beauty. Her blue eyes sparkled, her golden hair shone, and her sapphire silk dress glittered with the light of the crystal chandeliers. She moved with natural grace and elegance that bespoke good breeding.

It was no surprise she had captured his brother's attention. Jasper had always been drawn to beautiful women, especially those with fair coloring. He called them angelic. He would dance with them, take them driving in Hyde Park, and shower them with pretty posies—at least until his interest waned or was captured by another pair of blue eyes and golden locks. It had been the pattern for years now, ever since Jasper had finished at Eton. With his good looks and charisma, he'd always been able to charm most women.

Not long ago, their mother had asked Jasper if he planned to settle down at some point. He'd chortled, as though the mere suggestion was laughable, then insisted he had no intention of getting caught in the parson's noose anytime soon.

Yet here he was, recently returned from Gretna Green with a wife.

A wife.

Jasper had always been rash and impulsive, but this latest move had surprised even Morgan. Elopement? For what purpose, and why *this* blue-eyed angel over all the others? Two months ago, Jasper hadn't even known of Miss Abigail Nash's existence.

"A shilling for your thoughts," his mother spoke quietly at his side, startling Morgan. He hadn't heard her approach.

She waved a fan in front of her flushed face. The room was becoming unbearably hot, even with the open door.

Morgan took note of the new lines surrounding his mother's eyes and mouth and the creases in her forehead. Life had taken a toll on her of late. Ever since the passing of Morgan's father, the tell-tale signs of age had begun to manifest. In the light, Morgan could see a few gray streaks woven through the rich brown color of her hair.

She peered at him with an arched brow, patiently waiting for him to answer.

Morgan turned his attention back to the couple on the dance floor. "I was thinking they make a fine pair."

"They do," she agreed. "He is handsome, and she is quite lovely. Good breeding too, with a large dowry. Her father is on the continent at the moment. I had hoped he would return for the ball, but he sent his regrets. She has been staying with Lord and Lady Knave, who have overseen her launch into society."

Morgan nodded, already aware of his new sister-in-law's circumstances. He'd taken it upon himself to do his own sleuthing, not that it had enlightened him. If anything, what he'd learned only compounded his confusion.

"Why elope, Mother? They had no reason to. They both have excellent pedigrees, Jasper is well-situated, and she has a sizeable dowry. Neither family would have opposed the match."

"Since when has Jasper needed a reason to do anything?" asked his mother wryly. "He probably imbibed too much one evening, decided on a new lark, and convinced the poor girl it would be a grand adventure."

"Perhaps." Morgan had to concede that was the only explanation, but it didn't explain everything. His brother had always looked upon marriage as entrapment and elopement was not something society smiled upon, even when it came to a darling of the ton like Jasper. Despite his reckless ways, his brother had always valued his reputation.

There was also Miss Nash to consider. Why agree to the scheme? There had been no settlements negotiated on her behalf or agreements made. Her entire dowry would now belong to her new husband—a man who would spend it at the racetracks, gambling dens, Newmarket, or his tailor's. Jasper would also see his new wife provided for as well—he did have a heart, after all—but he had no head for business. He wouldn't care about investing or growing the sum. He would merely spend, spend, spend, and when the money ran dry, as was always the case with him, he'd look to Morgan for more.

Gads, would his bride be as daft?

"It's good the season is nearly over," said his mother. "By January, their elopement will be nothing more than a distant memory. Hopefully for me as well."

Morgan didn't need to ask the cause for her distress. It stemmed from a fortnight prior, when Jasper had breezed into the dining hall during dinner with a blushing Miss Nash on his arm. He'd announced that the lovely woman at his side should now be addressed as Lady Jasper Campbell. They'd just returned from Gretna Green, he'd said with a laugh, as though he had just returned from a day at the racetrack with his cronies.

Jasper hadn't bothered sending word ahead to prepare his mother, nor had he given anyone even a hint of his intentions. He'd merely disappeared for a few days as he often did, only this time, he didn't return bearing tales of various exploits and pranks. He'd returned with a wife.

His mother had remained stoically composed, at least until Jasper and Miss Nash—or rather, *Lady Jasper*—had retired for the evening. Only then did she wring her hands, berate her late husband for leaving her to deal with their ramshackle son alone, and sob on Morgan's shoulder. He'd comforted her as best he could while silently cursing his brother.

She'd eventually taken herself off to bed, and when morning came, bless her soul, she'd waltzed into the break-fast parlor with a stiff upper lip and a plan to throw an elaborate ball to celebrate the marriage of her son to Miss Abigail Nash.

Now here they were, hosting said ball in an effort to show the ton that the Campbell family thought nothing of the elopement and accepted the new Lady Jasper with open arms. From all appearances, it was a smashing success. Friends, family, and acquaintances had come in droves. But it didn't take a keen observer to notice the majority of on-lookers hadn't come to celebrate. They'd come to speculate.

Why an elopement? Why Miss Abigail Nash?

Morgan couldn't fault their curiosity, not when it mirrored his own.

"She doesn't have the glow one might expect from a new bride," his mother said.

Morgan peered closer at the couple, realizing that his mother spoke the truth. Although Lady Jasper smiled, laughed, and spoke to those she partnered, there was something forced in her expression. Peculiar that. She had once seemed quite taken with his brother.

Morgan still remembered the evening they'd met. Jasper had insisted his brother accompany him to Almack's to appease Sally Jersey, who wasn't happy with Morgan's lack of patronage. It had taken a great deal of convincing on Jasper's part—Morgan despised the top lofty setting—but he'd finally agreed, for no other reason than to quiet his brother. Not ten minutes after they had arrived, Jasper laid eyes on Miss Nash, begged Sally to introduce them, and had danced his first waltz of the evening.

Miss Nash had glowed then and again later that same evening, when Jasper had asked for a second dance. A few days later, she had blushed prettily when Japser bowed over her hand at Lady Mosley's musicale and had smiled blissfully a week later during a drive at Hyde Park, when Morgan had come upon the happy couple.

Looking at her now, however, there was no glimmer about her person. Rather, she appeared as though her mind was preoccupied with some distant, unpleasant memory. She hid it well—Morgan doubted others had noticed—but now that his mother had pointed it out, he could see it plainly.

She'd probably seen beyond her husband's charms to the shallowness beneath and was regretting her impulsiveness. Or perhaps she was mourning the loss of a grand wedding. An elopement may have sounded thrilling at one point, but certainly it had lost its allure by now.

Morgan shook his head. Marriage after only so short an acquaintance and an elopement at that?

Utter foolishness.

"Perhaps she is tired," his mother suggested, her furrowed brow belying her words.

"I'm sure that's it," Morgan agreed, hoping to ease her concerns. Since the passing of his father, she'd had enough burdens to fret over. She didn't need to worry that her younger son had landed himself in the worst sort of muddle, especially when there was nothing to be done at this point. Lord and Lady Jasper had made their choice. All the family could do now was put on a good face, throw a congratulatory ball, and embrace their new daughter and sister as best they could.

"She seems sweet," offered his mother.

"Yes."

"And she has an intelligent look about her. Perhaps she'll be a steadying influence on him."

Morgan had no reply to this. If the former Miss Nash had allowed Jasper to spirit her away to Gretna Green, how steadying or intelligent could she be? From all appearances, they were two peas in a pod—both handsome, impetuous, and foolish.

His mother examined her eldest son in that shrewd way he had come to loathe. After a moment, she sighed. "At least Jasper has finally married. I wasn't sure he ever would. Why aren't you dancing?"

"I find the quadrille tedious."

"The cotillion as well?" she asked, naming the dance that had come before the quadrille, which he'd also chosen to sit out.

"Yes."

"Surely there is at least one young lady present who interests you."

Morgan withheld an eye roll. They'd had this conversation before. "I made an effort at the beginning of the season, you know I did. I danced with many young ladies, called on several, and even took a few riding."

"I'm well aware," she said.

"Then you should also know that none of them captured my fancy."

"One might have, if you'd given her half a chance."

Morgan pushed away from the wall, not wishing to discuss his courting habits any longer. He fiddled with the cuff of his sleeve as he scanned the crowd, his gaze stopping on Miss Parker and her mischievous eyes. She grinned, encouraging him to approach with the promise of a diverting flirtation.

"Perhaps Miss Parker will partner me for the next dance. Will that meet with your approval, Mother?" Morgan knew full well it would not. The widowed father of Miss

Parker had attempted to court his mother while she was still in half mourning, and she'd yet to forgive the impertinence.

"You're punishing me," she said with a scowl.

"No, I am reminding you why I have not settled on a bride as of yet. Miss Parker is the most interesting debutante I have become acquainted with this season."

"Fiddlesticks."

Morgan pulled his gloves tighter around his fingers and lowered his voice to a murmur. "*She* did not attempt to court you, Mother. Her father did."

"At her encouragement, or so I've been told."

He lifted an eyebrow. "You've never been one to listen to gossip."

"It's not gossip when it comes from a close friend who isn't prone to embellishment."

Morgan refrained from pointing out that his mother was still young and beautiful. It was only natural for a man like Mr. Parker to wish to court her. Granted, he ought to have waited out her mourning period, but worse crimes had been committed.

"Why would Miss Parker encourage her father to court you?" asked Morgan.

The look his mother gave him said he should already know the answer. "Isn't it obvious? If I were to marry her father, it would place her in a better position to sink her clutches into you. It's no secret she has set her cap at you. Look at her now. She has kept one eye on you all evening."

Morgan glanced at Miss Parker again. The moment their gazes locked, her eyes crinkled flirtatiously, only now her smile appeared more cunning than mischievous.

Morgan's neckcloth felt restrictive all of a sudden, so he tugged on it and took a step closer to the door.

"Ah, see?" said his mother in an amused tone. "You don't wish to be entrapped any more than I do."

Morgan forced his hand back to his side, thinking his mother was far too perceptive. Over the past few years, the seasons had begun to feel like a game of chess, with mothers and daughters making calculated moves to break through his defenses and capture him. It unnerved him. He had no intention of marrying a conniving woman. He wanted some-one real. Someone he could trust. Someone who enjoyed his company as much as he did hers.

He had to hand it to Miss Parker, though. She had been more subtle than the rest. Up until now, Morgan had considered her to be a diverting dance partner, nothing more. Now he knew better.

The quadrille came to an end, and Morgan made a quick decision. "Perhaps I will request a dance from my new sister-in-law instead."

"How very cowardly of you," teased his mother.

"Not cowardly. Strategic," he said before moving forward to claim the hand of a woman who wouldn't be out to ensnare him. How she'd managed to snare his brother was the question.

As he approached, Lord and Lady Knave did as well. They were an attractive pair who'd endured their own share of gossip—something about Lady Knave stealing her sister's intended or Lord Knave marrying the younger Gifford daughter because he'd been spurned by the elder? Morgan didn't know which version was closer to the truth, nor did he care. However their union came about, it seemed a happy one. He simply wanted to know why they hadn't kept a closer eye on their charge.

"Lord and Lady Knave." Morgan nodded to both in turn. "I see you are acquainted with my new sister-in-law."

Lady Knave tucked her arm through Lady Jasper's. "Your brother has absconded with my dearest friend, sir, and I cannot decide if I should be pleased or irate with him."

"Jasper has that effect on most, I'm afraid," said Morgan wryly.

Jasper took his wife's hand and brought it to his lips. "You should only ever be pleased, Lady Knave. I adore this woman and could not wait another moment to make her mine. How fortunate am I that she agreed."

Lady Jasper blushed prettily. "I am the fortunate one, my lord." Her words were spoken without flippancy, but there was also some hesitancy, as though she meant them but didn't at the same time. How very peculiar.

"Lord Brigston, if you have come to request a dance from Lady Jasper, you are too late," Lady Knave said, interrupting his thoughts. "My husband has already secured her hand for the minuet."

This seemed to surprise both her husband and Lady Jasper, but they were quick to mask it behind smiles.

Jasper didn't seem to notice the exchange. He took the news good-naturedly, tucking his wife's arm possessively through his own. "I'm not sure I can part with my wife, even for you, Lord Knave. Must you dance with him, my dear?" His eyes twinkled as he gazed down at her. She was a head shorter than him, which meant she would only be a half a head shorter than Morgan. His brother had always had the larger personality, and at some point during their adolescent years, he had gained the larger stature as well.

"It isn't fashionable to dote on one's wife, my lord," said Lady Jasper.

"It isn't fashionable to elope either, yet here we are."

"Which is why we should not give the gossips more to discuss." She gently retracted her arm and curtsied to Lord Knave. "I would be honored to dance with you, my lord."

"You used to call me Knave," he said as he held out his arm.

Her smile appeared weary. "Forgive me, Knave. I am not quite myself this evening."

"Would you prefer to rest this set instead? You are looking a trifle pale." His brow crinkled in concern.

"And miss the opportunity to dance with a dear friend? I think not."

Morgan kept an eye on the pair as they walked to the dance floor. He couldn't deny that his sister-in-law made a graceful figure next to Lord Knave. The alluring swing of her hips, her straight posture, and the elegant curve of her neck would capture most men's attention. For his brother's sake, Morgan hoped there was more to her than beauty.

"Lord Jasper," said Lady Knave, pulling his brother's— and Morgan's—attention back to her. "I wonder if you would be so kind as to procure me some punch? I'm feeling parched all of a sudden."

"Your wish is my command." Jasper gallantly bowed before excusing himself.

As soon as he was out of earshot, Lady Knave stepped beside Morgan and took his arm. "Lord Brigston, I have been watching you for much of the evening, and I believe that you are as bewildered and troubled about this elopement as I am. Have I deduced your feelings accurately?"

He hesitated a span before answering. "Yes."

She nodded. "I assure you we had no notion they were planning to elope. Lord Jasper arranged for them to see the fireworks at Vauxhall with a large party, and we assumed her reputation would be safe with him. He didn't send word of their actual destination until the following morning. By then it was too late to follow. I'm sorry for it." She frowned, and glanced sideways at Jasper, who had stopped to converse with an older woman. "I do not know your brother well, but he seems to be a decent sort of person. Please tell me I am correct in that deduction as well."

Morgan had never been spoken to in such a forthright manner by a woman he hardly knew. As refreshing as candor was to artifice, it made him uncomfortable.

"What makes you think you can trust my opinion, Lady Knave?" he asked.

She met his gaze. "My father-in-law tells me you speak your opinions plainly and intelligently in the House of Lords. I'm hoping you'll do the same with me."

Only a few moments remained before Jasper returned, but Morgan didn't know how to answer. He couldn't exactly say his brother was a fool, but he couldn't lie either.

He chose his words carefully. "Jasper is impetuous, at times heedless, and prefers to live in the moment without giving much thought to the consequences. But his spirits are always high, and he has a good heart. I believe he will make your friend an admirable husband." Morgan could only hope that would be the case. Jasper had it in him to be a good husband if that's what he chose to be.

Lady Knave nodded slowly, no doubt contemplating his words. In the end, she seemed satisfied by his answer. "Thank you for being candid with me, Lord Brigston. I was aware that Abby nursed a tendré for your brother, but I haven't the faintest notion what induced them to marry in such a ramshackle fashion. As she mentioned earlier, she has not been herself since their return, not even with me. There is a distance between us that has never existed before, and I don't understand it."

"I wish I could enlighten you, my lady."

She frowned and plucked at the fingertips of her gloves. "What's done is done, I suppose, and it relieves my mind to know she has wed a good man. I hope they will find happiness together, I truly do." She pressed her lips together before adding, "I cannot force her to confide in me, but if she should find herself in need of a friend at some point, know that I would come in an instant."

"I believe you would," said Morgan, impressed by her perception and thoughtfulness. The new Lady Jasper must have some redeeming qualities if she'd manage to acquire such a dedicated and loyal friend. Jasper's cronies were certainly not of the same caliber.

Lady Knave continued to fiddle with her gloves, so Morgan touched her shoulder in a gesture of comfort. "I'm certain you're worrying needlessly, my lady."

"I can only pray that I am," she murmured.

Seconds later, when Jasper returned with her requested glass of punch, all creases around her eyes vanished as she flashed him a winsome smile. "Thank you, kind sir. You have been most prompt."

"I would never keep such a lovely lady waiting for too long, especially in this stifling room." He waved a hand in front of his face. "Am I alone in thinking it excessively warm in here?"

Lady Knave took a sip of her drink. "Hopefully you do not think it too warm to dance, Lord Jasper. I hear you make an . . . *admirable* partner." She cast a meaningful glance at Morgan before dimpling at his brother.

Jasper took her half-empty glass and handed it off to a passing footman. "If Morgan has given you the impression that my dancing skills are only admirable, he has led you astray. I challenge you to find another man in this room who can dance the steps of the minuet with as much dexterity and finesse as I."

Her eyes sparkled with delight as she accepted his arm. "Challenge accepted, my lord."

Morgan couldn't resist a smile of his own as they walked away. Something told him that his brother wouldn't be exchanging pleasantries with Lady Knave. She was on a mission to see that her friend would be happily situated, and Morgan would wager a large sum that Jasper was about to be measured and interrogated. Perhaps even lectured.

No one could be more deserving.

TWO

Two Months Later

A KNOCK ON the door caused Morgan to look up from his estate ledgers. He cast a quick glance at his bailiff, Mr. Decker, who sat across from him. The man was short, somewhat gaunt, and rarely smiled, but he performed his duties admirably. Morgan had relied on his wise counsel since the death of his father.

"Enter," called Morgan.

The door opened, and his butler, Smithson, walked in, his commanding height making the room feel smaller. He knew better than to disturb his employer during a business meeting, so the reason for his interruption had to be important.

"What is it, Smithson?" he asked.

"Forgive the intrusion, my lord, but your mother has asked that I summon you to the drawing room. Lord and Lady Jasper have arrived."

Morgan took a moment to digest the news. Jasper? Here? Now? Why? His brother despised Oakley Grange. The village of Cawley boasted only a small society, which Jasper found sadly wanting. He preferred the hustle and bustle of town during the season and Brighton the remainder of the year, with various house parties in betwixt and between. During the past five years, Jasper had returned to Oakley Grange only twice. Once, to host a hunting party and the other to attend their father's funeral, not that Morgan was complaining. Jasper's presence often had a disruptive influence on Morgan's life, and while he exercised patience with his brother in town, he preferred to be left alone at Oakley.

"Did my brother mention how long he intends to stay?" Morgan glanced at Mr. Decker again, knowing he would be expected to entertain his brother, dine with the family, and waste precious hours socializing. He didn't have the time or the desire to engage in such pursuits.

"No, my lord," answered the butler, "but they brought several trunks with them."

In other words, they'd come prepared for a lengthy stay. *Blast.*

Morgan stood and walked to the window, looking out over the western side of his property. There was much to be done during the next few months and so little time to do it. His family had been using the same open-field system for years. Not long after Morgan had stepped into the title of Marquess of Brigston, he had decided it was past time to join the strips of common fields into larger, organized areas, and enclose them with hedgerows of hawthorn and copse wood. Many other estates had enclosed their fields, and the benefits were immense. It would aid in crop rotation and provide designated grazing areas for cattle—another investment Morgan planned to tackle in the near future.

Unfortunately, his plans required a significant investment of both capital and time, the latter of which did not please his mother. Only yesterday, she'd accused him of becoming too consumed with his new role and forgetting about other, equally important duties, such as finding a wife and settling down. But Morgan wasn't interested in courting or taking on a wife just yet. He was interested in renovation and bringing the family's estate into the nineteenth century with all possible speed.

But now that Jasper had arrived . . . Morgan's hopes of accomplishing everything before the next parliament session began to dissolve.

"I can't imagine it will be for too long," Smithson added, probably noting the frustration on his employer's face. "Your brother does not like to linger in the country for long."

"Unless he has invited some cronies for a house party," muttered Morgan under his breath, praying that wasn't the case. He turned away from the window and eyed his ledgers, wishing he could ignore his brother and return to work.

His mother would never forgive him.

Morgan sighed. "Mr. Decker, it seems we must postpone this meeting for another time. Please excuse me."

"Of course, my lord."

Morgan stepped into the hallway and followed the sound of voices to the drawing room. His brother was recounting a tale, probably about their journey to Oakley. With Jasper, there was always a tale.

He paused outside the room, waiting for his brother to finish.

"A herd of cows blocked the road, impeding our progress. Our coachman yelled and waved his arms, to no avail. The stubborn beasts would not budge. While I hunted around for a nice spot under some trees where Lady Jasper and I could wait in some comfort, she had other plans. She located a long stick and began whipping the backsides of those wretched cows, telling them to get a move on."

Jasper chortled. "I had no idea I had married such a determined woman, but wouldn't you know, those beasts at last began to move. Even our coachman couldn't hide his astonishment. I have never been so diverted in my life."

"Oh my," said their mother, sounding more shocked than diverted.

Morgan hid his smile as he entered the room, making his presence known.

"There you are, Morgan." His mother cast him a grateful look. "Only look who has come. Isn't it wonderful?"

"Yes." He nodded to the newcomers. Jasper appeared his usual, well-kept self, but his wife's bonnet was slightly askew, a few wayward strands of hair had escaped her coiffure, and the hem of her dusty blue skirt was marred with blotches of mud. Apparently, the cows had found a way to settle the score somewhat.

"Welcome, Jasper and . . . Lady Jasper." Morgan wasn't sure he'd ever get used to the sound of that name.

"Please call me Abby," she implored. "We are brother and sister, after all. I would rather not stand on ceremony."

Jasper took her hand possessively in his and grinned. "She has entreated me to do the same, but I refuse. She is a lady in every way, and I cannot call her anything less."

"A lady who whips cows?" she asked wryly. "I've never heard of such a thing."

Morgan snickered but quickly covered it up with a cough. He may not know his new sister-in-law well, but he liked that she didn't take herself, or her new title, too seriously.

Jasper pressed a kiss to her fingers. "Only a lady would take charge as you did, my dear. I thought it most commanding of you."

"You exaggerate." Red tinged her cheeks, and she

shifted uncomfortably. "Impatience led me to act as I did, not command. I had no wish to sit among the weeds and wait it out."

Morgan would have felt the same. Passing time beneath a tree might sound romantic, but the ground would have been uneven and hard, the grass itchy, and the bugs irritating. Rather than brandish a stick at the cows, however, Morgan would have been more inclined to unhitch a horse, borrow the coachman's whip, and encourage the herd to move from atop a taller beast.

"Were you not afraid of getting trampled?" asked Lady Brigston.

Abby shook her head. "My father raised cattle, and I've become accustomed to them. Sometimes our caretaker would let me accompany him when he'd have to check on something in the fields. It was great fun."

His mother's eyes grew wider by the moment. "Your father allowed you to round up cattle with the help?"

Abby blushed, looking as though she regretted speaking so openly. "Er . . . no. Not exactly. He was away much of the time for business, and . . . well, I suppose that what he didn't know he couldn't scold me for later."

Jasper laughed while his mother attempted to hide her astonishment behind a distressed smile. She had always been a stickler for rules and conventions. If she'd ever had a daughter, Morgan was certain that an afternoon spent rounding up cattle wouldn't have been an option.

Abby fiddled with her leather traveling gloves, which she now held on her lap. Since Jasper seemed oblivious to his wife's discomfort, Morgan attempted to set her at ease.

"I would like to speak with your father one day, Abby. I have been considering investing in some cattle and would love to hear his opinion on the matter. Has it been a successful venture for him, do you know?"

She brightened a little. "I believe so. He rarely spoke of such things to me, but he must have considered it worthwhile because we were never without cows. If you'd like, I can write to him on your behalf, Lord Brigston."

"If I am to call you Abby, you must call me Brigston. I'd rather not stand on ceremony either. And yes, I would be grateful for an introduction."

Jasper settled against the back of the settee and stretched his arms as though bored.

"If you will write down the questions you have," Abby offered, "I will send them with my letter."

"Thank you. Tell me, did he keep bulls as well?"

She nodded, and a few more curls escaped from beneath her bonnet. She quickly swept them behind her ear as she made a face. "Unfortunately, yes. Cows may be docile creatures, but bulls are not. I was charged once as a girl, and I had to scramble under the fence to get away from the horrid creature. I can still see the cruel gleam in his black eyes."

Her words must have piqued Jasper's interest because he returned to the conversation. "I'm certain my brother would never invest in such creatures, my love, at least not while you're at Oakley."

Jasper was doing it a bit brown, even for Jasper. Morgan barely refrained from rolling his eyes. "I don't have immediate plans to acquire cattle, but when I do, a bull will be a necessary evil, I'm afraid. One cannot breed cattle without them."

"Morgan, how can you speak of such things with ladies present?" chided his mother. Morgan might have felt penitent if Abby had not ducked her head to hide a smile. Good. Now she wouldn't be the only one to cause shock and appall.

"Forgive me, Mother and Abby," he said.

"What about me?" teased Jasper. "Do you not have a care for my sensibilities as well?"

"I can't say that I do," said Morgan.

Jasper brushed some dust from his pantaloons and shook his head sadly at his bride. "Can you now see the torment I've been made to endure? Morgan has always been an unfeeling brother. If I had not been blessed with such an angelic mother, I would have become wretched indeed."

Morgan nodded in agreement. "Without Mother's influence, you'd likely be in prison for stealing the Carthright's horse and trying to convince Danny Jones that oak sap was honey."

Jasper smiled smugly, no doubt proud of his misadventures. "I only borrowed that horse, and Danny deserved that sap for destroying the fort I built on the beach."

"You mean the fort *Father and I* built," said Morgan dryly. "Oh wait, you did drag over that one log, didn't you? So you'd have a place to sit and watch us work."

Jasper cocked his head at his wife. "My brother has a dreadful memory."

"And you have an inflated opinion of yourself," said Morgan.

"Good heavens," their mother inserted. "Do you want Abby to think you're both rogues?" She tried to mask her amusement behind a look of chastisement but failed. It was obvious she was enjoying the banter, probably because it was a rare occurrence. Though the brothers had been close at one time, the passing years had forced a divide between them. Morgan had become more responsible while Jasper dallied about, heedless of anyone's desires but his own.

There was a reason the brothers were no longer close.

"Abby, who looked after you while your father was

away?" his mother asked, no doubt attempting to bring her daughter-in-law back into the conversation.

"My great-aunt Josephine. She was older and . . . inclined to snooze a great deal."

Morgan pressed his lips together to avoid smiling. Abby was proving to be highly diverting. Not many would dare admit as much to the dowager marchioness, but Abby made no apologies for her father or the way she was raised. Morgan had to give her credit for that. Perhaps there was more to his new sister-in-law than met the eye. Perhaps his brother had seen it too, and this marriage had not been as impulsive as it seemed.

"Did your father not employ a governess?" pressed his mother.

"My great-aunt Josephine came to us as my governess. In the beginning, she was adept and taught me well, but during my fourteenth year, she suffered an apoplexy and was never the same. She would fade away now and again, and her memory wasn't as sharp. Over time, she began to nap more and instruct less, and when my father at last realized the full extent of her illness, I had grown accustomed to my independence and pled with him not to replace her. He reluctantly agreed when I assured him I would study on my own—which I did, but I also let myself enjoy life more."

She eyed her mother-in-law with nervousness. "I hope that doesn't come as a shock to you, Lady Brigston."

"Not at all," she replied weakly.

Jasper must have finally noticed his wife's discomfort because he stood and held a hand out to her. "Forgive us, but Lady Jasper and I would like to get some rest before dinner. It has been a long journey."

"Of course," said their mother. "I'll ring for Mrs. Willows, and she can show you to your rooms."

Abby dipped into a quick curtsy. "Thank you, Lady Brigston, for welcoming us with such kindness. You as well, Lord—er, Brigston."

Morgan propped his elbow on the mantle until the housekeeper led them from the room. He would have returned to his study if not for the anxious look on his mother's face. She sat down on a chair near him and fretted over her lower lip.

The ledgers would have to wait a bit longer. "What is troubling you, Mother?"

She clasped her hands together and furrowed her brow. "I only wonder if Abby is prepared to be a wife. Jasper will expect her to host hunting parties, soirées, picnics, and balls. You know him. He is a sociable creature. Does she know how to manage a house and servants? Does she know how to compose invitations or plan a menu? Does she know anything about finances or the proper way to hire and train servants? Does she know what charitable acts and contributions are expected of her? Good heavens, does she even attend church services? What sort of woman has my son married? One cannot whip an insubordinate servant like one would a cow."

"I'm sure she knows that, Mother," said Morgan, but she didn't seem to hear him.

"How could her father allow her to be raised in that way, and why would he relegate such an important responsibility as her come out to a newly married friend instead of overseeing it himself? He didn't even trouble himself to attend her marriage ball!"

She grew more irate by the moment, so Morgan took a seat across from her and captured her hands. "He's on the continent, and don't forget he's a widower. A man can only do so much without a wife at his side."

"I know, but that is no excuse to neglect her in such a fashion. At the very least, he should have employed a proper governess, kept her away from cattle, and educated her on the foolishness of elopement."

Morgan couldn't argue those points, but he wouldn't agree with them either, not when it would exacerbate his mother's anxiety. "Abby has not been blessed with a mother like you, but from what I have observed thus far, she carries herself well, she seems to know what is expected of her in public, and she speaks intelligently. Perhaps she doesn't know her way around a household as you do, but she is now your daughter-in-law, is she not? There is no one better equipped to instruct her than you."

His mother's distress eventually gave way to something resembling determination. She sat up straighter, and her brow cleared. "You are right, Morgan. Like it or not, Abby *is* my daughter-in-law, and if she is brazen enough to whip cows to do her bidding, with the right tutelage, perhaps she can bring Jasper around."

Morgan leaned back in his chair, stretching his arms behind his head. "Don't expect a miracle, Mother."

"Don't *you* underestimate the power of a woman's influence. Your father was somewhat of a rascal when we met."

"Yet you married him anyway."

"Only because I saw a man with a great deal of po-tential. That, and his smile made me go weak at the knees." She smiled. It was a rare thing to see these days, and Morgan was happy to be a witness. It made him glad he'd set his ledgers aside for a time.

"The truth is," his mother continued, "your father influenced me as much as I did him. I may have been raised by more attentive parents than Abby, but when I married, I was still young, naive, and unprepared in many ways. I need to remember that and not judge her too harshly. Time and experience is all she requires."

"She needs you as well," he added.

"I shall be glad to help however I can."

With that settled, Morgan stood and adjusted the sleeves of his coat. "You'll have to excuse me as well. I have some matters to attend to."

She waved a dismissive hand at him. "Go. Attend to your business for now. But I expect you to be on time for dinner and not disappear afterwards. I am glad Jasper and Abby have come. With you as busy as you have been of late, Oakley Grange has become far too quiet. We could use some liveliness."

As Morgan returned to his study, he thought over his mother's words, wondering if his obsession with his estate had made him too self-absorbed. He had to concede that he hadn't given much thought to his mother since their return from town. She always seemed in good spirits and had a small circle of friends in the vicinity. But was she truly happy? It seemed she missed her husband and children more than she let on.

Perhaps it was time to put his concerns about his brother aside and be grateful for his arrival as well. No one could ever feel lonely with Jasper around.

THREE

LESS THAN A week later, gulls chirped outside the study's window, providing a cheerful accompaniment to Morgan's less-than-cheerful discussion with his bailiff. Apparently, one of the parcels of land they were attempting to enclose was not draining as they hoped it would. A ditch would be needed to keep the southernmost part free from muck, but that meant dissecting another field or redesigning parcels— both of which Morgan was loathe to do. They were already behind schedule and didn't have time to reconfigure anything.

Blast, blast, blast.

A rap on the door interrupted them, and Morgan swallowed another curse. *Not now.*

The door opened without permission, and Jasper walked in, raising a brow. "Business again, brother? Do you never let it rest? Only look out the window and see the beautiful morning that awaits."

Morgan leaned back in his chair and glanced at the clock on the mantle, raising a brow. "You mean afternoon, don't you?"

Jasper settled himself into a large chair near the fireplace and interlocked his fingers across his waistcoat. He was dressed as though he were still in town. Gray pantaloons, slightly darker coat, black Hessians, crisp white shirt, and a blue waistcoat. At least he didn't appear flamboyant. Jasper might surround himself with dandies, but he never dressed like one. Still, Morgan wondered if he owned a pair of buckskins or even some comfortable trousers.

"I have never understood country hours," said Jasper in a bored fashion. "Why rise early when it is so much colder inside and out? I find it's best to stay buried in my bed clothes until the sun has warmed things up a bit."

"We have fireplaces in every room," said Morgan.

"Yes, but a small fire in the grate has no effect on the outside air, does it? I require a morning ride to get my heart beating, and I prefer warmer air."

"You mean an afternoon ride."

Jasper sighed and examined his fingers. "We are back to that, are we? How tiring you can be at times."

Morgan dropped his quill on the enclosure plans and folded his arms. He and Mr. Decker would not reach any sort of consensus on the matter of the ditch until they had rid themselves of Jasper. "Do you need something, brother, or are you merely seeking refuge in one of the warmer rooms in the house?"

"Now that you mention it, the temperature *is* pleasing in here," Jasper said.

"You'll find the library just as pleasing, if not more so."

Jasper grimaced. "And surround myself with all those dusty books? Thank you, no. I'd as lief spend the day in a mausoleum."

Morgan glanced pointedly at the bookcase stuffed with books not far from where Jasper sat. "You find the study more to your liking?"

Another grimace. "Gads no. But I knew you were shut

away again and probably wouldn't surface until dinner. Since I'd like a private word with you before then, I had no other recourse than to seek you out." He sniffed the air and frowned. "It smells so old in here."

Morgan rolled his eyes and looked at his bailiff. "I do apologize, Mr. Decker, but it seems we'll need to postpone yet another meeting." This was becoming a habit—one Morgan could do without.

"Very good, my lord. I will be at my desk when you are ready to continue." His bailiff slid the quill aside and rolled up the plans, taking them with him.

Morgan had to remind himself that his mother had been a great deal happier of late, due mostly to Jasper's presence. If his brother required a private word, Morgan would comply.

"What is it you wish to speak with me about?"

Jasper examined his shirt cuffs with a frown, as though he'd found a smudge. He brushed at the spot. "I am hoping you will look after Lady Jasper for a week or so. A fortnight at the most."

Morgan's jaw clenched. He should have expected this. His brother could never stay at Oakley for long. "Are you going somewhere?"

"Just a short jaunt to Oxfordshire. My friend is hosting a grouse hunt at the beginning of September and has asked that I help scout out the best locations."

Which meant a fortnight would turn into a month or more. Jasper wouldn't be content to leave before the hunt began.

"Is there a reason you aren't taking Abby with you? Surely there will be other women present."

"Lady Jasper is . . . indisposed and would prefer to remain here." Even though Abby had repeatedly asked her husband to call her by her given name, he persisted in referring to her as Lady Jasper, probably because he liked hearing his own name spoken. It irked Morgan. He wanted to respect his sister-in-law's wishes, but it felt increasingly intimate to call her Abby while her husband used her title.

Jasper had always been annoyingly stubborn.

"Is she ill?" Morgan asked, not sure he believed it. Abby had seemed in perfect health only last evening when she had played a lovely sonata on the pianoforte. She had struggled through a few measures, and Morgan noticed his mother wincing at times, but overall, she'd performed admirably.

"Er . . . not exactly," Jasper said.

Morgan was quickly losing patience with his brother. "How can a person be *not exactly* indisposed? Either she is or she isn't."

"She's breeding," Jasper blurted. He jumped up from the chair and walked to the window, gripping his beaver hat tightly in his hands as he stared into the distance, his jaw taut.

Morgan opened his mouth to respond but he had no idea what to say. It was a rare occurrence to see his brother shaken. Morgan could remember only a handful of times that Jasper had discarded flippancy for something more serious. Their father's funeral had been one of those times. Jasper hadn't said a word. He'd merely stood still, watching the casket disappear beneath mounds of earth. When the last shovelful had been thrown, he'd turned around and walked away. Morgan hadn't seen him again until the following morning when Jasper's usual levity had returned.

He'd never forget his brother's parting words that day. "Pray you never die before you sire a son, brother. Should this property ever fall into my hands, I would sell it and purchase Newmarket instead."

"It's entailed," said Morgan. "You cannot sell it. Why not turn it into a racetrack instead?"

Jasper brightened. "Now there's a thought, not that I am wishing you to the grave, of course. Funerals are far too tedious. But if it should ever come to that, a racetrack might be just the thing. I might suggest that you take the initiative if I didn't already know that you would never consider it."

"You seem to know me better than I know you these days. Try as I might, I can't understand why you are so repulsed by a home you used to love."

"I wouldn't say repulsed," Jasper said as he tugged on his gloves. "I've simply outgrown it."

Morgan nearly asked how a person outgrew a large estate, but what good would it do when his brother had no vested interest in the property? Entails went from father to the eldest son. Younger sons were expected to find their way elsewhere. Perhaps if the birth order had been reversed, Morgan would feel the same. He couldn't fault his brother for not caring about Oakley when he had no reason to do so.

Perhaps that's why he stayed away, why he now felt the need to go off on some hunting excursion and leave his wife behind—his *expectant* wife.

Morgan could hardly believe it. Jasper had actually fathered a child, a feat Morgan and his mother never thought would happen, at least not a legitimate child. It seemed his younger brother had surpassed him in both height and duty.

Gads, his mother would have something to say about that.

"Has she seen a doctor?" Morgan asked.

Jasper shook his head. "She refused to let me summon anyone until you and Mother had been informed of the situation."

"Does Mother know?"

31

Jasper cleared his throat and turned away from the window. "I have decided to let you do the honors. Mother will be ecstatic."

"Which begs the question: Why not tell her yourself? You have always enjoyed crowing to a captive audience."

"I don't have the time. The carriage is being loaded as we speak, and Mother is off making morning calls or tending to a sick tenant somewhere."

"You are leaving *now*?" Morgan rose and leaned over his desk, planting his palms on the wooden surface. "You will not even wait for the doctor to arrive?"

Jasper swallowed. "I told you. I am not at liberty to summon him until Mother has been informed."

Morgan stared at his brother, trying to piece together this latest news along with everything else. "In other words, you would like me to summon the doctor and see to your wife's health while you go gallivanting across the country to shoot some birds."

Jasper had the grace to appear rueful. His shoulders drooped as he turned away. "Abby understands. She knows I have reached my limit and cannot remain in this silent house any longer. I feel as though I'm going mad."

Morgan closed his eyes and drew in a deep breath, trying to calm his rising anger. He had only just assumed his brother stayed away because Oakley didn't belong to him, but maybe there was more to it than that. Maybe his brother needed more than Oakley could offer. If so, what did that mean for Morgan and Abby and their mother? Was this how the next year would unfold? Jasper leaving every chance he could and returning only when absolutely necessary? Would Morgan be expected to oversee the raising of Jasper's child as well?

And what of Abby? Did she really understand why her

husband was leaving her in the hands of near strangers? They were family, yes, but the relationship was too recent to really claim any sort of bond or kinship.

"I know what you must think of me," said Jasper, in a rare moment of contrition.

"You have no idea what I'm thinking."

"You think I'm shirking my responsibilities, but you don't understand."

"What don't I understand?"

Jasper shook his head and ran his fingers through his short crop of curls. Morgan wondered if he would finally get an honest answer from his brother—one not laced with sarcasm or flippancy. But when his brother locked gazes with him once more, the cloak of distance had returned. "It's not something I can explain to you. I . . . need to go."

He started towards the door until Morgan's voice stopped him. "When do you expect to return? And I mean *truly* return?"

A pause and then, "I can't say for certain, only that I will. I do care for Abby, you know."

The door opened, and Jasper disappeared through it. Morgan had the greatest urge to chase him down and accuse him of being the coward of all cowards, but it would do no good to throw out accusations. His brother had already made up his mind, and no ranting about would change it. He could only hope Jasper would follow through on his promise to return and that Abby would not be made to suffer as a result.

With a sigh, Morgan dropped to his chair and ran his hands over his face, thinking the problem with the ditch was simple in comparison.

If only one could choose one's relatives.

FOUR

ABBY PAUSED WHERE seawater met pebbly sand and tilted her face to the sunny sky above. She breathed in the salty air, feeling the breeze whip at her skirts and cool her neck. It had been unusually warm the past few weeks, ever since Jasper had gone. When she had first come to Oakley, she would rise early and wander through the gardens and surrounding woods, but gradually, her feet had carried her towards the ocean breezes, and she ended up on the beach. Since that time, she'd returned every day.

Having lived most of her life in Oxfordshire, Abby had never seen the ocean before. It entranced her. The humid air, the sound of water lapping at the shoreline, the rocky sand beneath her feet. She'd removed her boots and stockings and now squished her toes through the larger pebbles to the softer sand beneath. It felt liberating, like directing cows or cantering through the woods on the back of a horse.

Abby took several steps closer to the sea and smiled when the cool water washed over her feet. What would it feel like to continue walking forward until the water reached her waist? How would it be to pick up her feet and let it carry her along? Was it difficult to swim?

If only she'd learned.

She lifted her skirts, but only a little. She didn't mind them somewhat damp. It served to cool her on the long trek back to the house, although her maid, Evie, would click her tongue in that disapproving way as soon as she spied the dirt. Abby might feel the same if she was required to wash and mend her own clothes, but for now, she luxuriated in the feel of the cool, wet fabric. It added extra weight, to be sure, but that was a feeling she would need to get used to eventually.

She placed her hand over her belly and thought of the small life growing inside of her. Everything felt surreal. Marriage. Jasper. A babe. Could this truly be her life? A little over six months ago, she'd arrived in London with breathless anticipation. She had dreamed of dancing with scores of handsome men, attending the theater, learning to waltz, enlarging her wardrobe with the latest fashions, and tasting the famous ices at Gunter's. She'd even experienced that life for a while, but in the span of one night, everything had changed.

Careless decisions came back to haunt her, stealing her fantasies and landing her squarely in a changed reality of her own making. It wasn't that her life was dreadful, by any means, but she felt cheated, as though she'd been forced to take a step she hadn't been ready to take. She hadn't wanted this, not yet, and she knew Jasper hadn't either. He would never admit as much, but every so often, she could see loss in his eyes.

Where was he at this moment? Did he miss her? Was he regretting his impulsive decision to spirit her off to Gretna Green? How could he not?

Abby shouldn't have been swayed by his charms or agreed to his plan. She should have pushed him away and endured the consequences of her decisions alone. It would have been the right thing to do, the selfless thing.

It also would have ruined her.

The sound of pounding hooves caught her attention, and she looked up to see a horse and rider careening down the beach at full speed, stirring up the sand and leaving a cloud of dust behind. Even though she couldn't see the details of the man's face, she recognized the way he rode low over his horse's head with reckless elegance.

Abby had seen Brigston riding often over the past several weeks—either from the window in her bedchamber or while she was out walking the grounds. She was usually careful to stay out of his way, hiding behind a curtain, tree, or hedge, so they rarely encountered one another, but there was nothing to hide behind now. She couldn't exactly dive into the waves or make a run for the hedges in the distance. How silly that would look.

Abby backed away from the water, dug her toes into the sand to bury them, and tucked her hands behind her back, keeping her stockings and boots out of sight. With any luck, he'd merely nod or wave and continue on, but he slowed his horse and stopped not far from where she stood. He wore no hat, and his wavy, sandy hair fell across his forehead in a reckless fashion. He didn't look much like a marquess at the moment. Rather, his casual attire and shorter, solid frame reminded her of the men who'd worked in her father's stables.

He studied her with his stormy gray eyes, probably taking in her damp skirts and unkempt hair. At least she'd left her bonnet intact. He couldn't find fault with her there.

"You are out and about early this morning, Abby," he remarked.

"I usually am," she said. "Once the sun awakens, so do I."

She pressed her feet a little further into the sand, hoping

he wouldn't notice her lack of stockings. He had always been kind to her, but she had never felt comfortable in his presence, and being here alone with him, especially in her current state of undress, unnerved her more than usual.

His eyes crinkled at the corners, and he smiled wryly. "Are you hiding your stockings and boots behind your back?"

The question startled her, and it took a moment to gather her wits. She squared her shoulders, keeping her hands hidden. "I don't know what you mean, sir. I would never remove my boots or stockings out of doors."

"Only indoors then? While at dinner, perhaps?"

"I was referring to my bedchamber, as you well know."

He was teasing her in a way that Jasper might have done. Her husband had only been gone a fortnight, but there were times, such as now, that she missed him—perhaps not in the way a wife should miss her husband, but Abby felt more at ease with him.

Brigston guided his horse a few steps to the right, trying to peek behind her, but Abby countered by moving to the left, keeping her hands hidden.

"'Tis a shame, that," he mused. "There is nothing as invigorating as dipping one's feet in the ocean. You ought to try it sometime."

"I think your mother would be scandalized to hear you suggest such a thing," said Abby, wishing he'd move along.

"No more scandalized than she'd be to see you now, attempting to hide your footwear behind your back."

Abby gave up trying to counter his movements and scowled instead. "How unkind you are to call my bluff, sir." She brought her boots forward, holding them up for his inspection. Thankfully her stockings were stuffed inside and out of sight. "Are you happy to have uncovered another one of my flaws? Pray do not tell your mother. She thinks me hoyden enough already."

He chuckled. "Never fear, sister. You have found a kindred spirit in me. I, too, enjoy wading in the water."

He swung down from his horse and collected the reins in his gloved hands, his close proximity making her shy away a step. It was a silly reaction. She had no reason to fear him, but he still made her anxious. Perhaps, in time, that feeling would subside, as it had with Jasper, but for now, she would greatly prefer that Brigston keep his distance.

Why had she asked that he call her Abby, and why did she call him Brigston? It felt too friendly by half.

She cleared her throat. "I was just contemplating what it would feel like to swim. Does that shock you?" She hoped it would.

"Not at all," he said. "Jasper and I had the same notion when we were lads and even begged our father to teach us to swim. He obliged as he always did, and the three of us spent many hours in the sea. At one point, Jasper and I even tried to construct a boat from logs before we learned we had no talent for lashing."

Abby smiled a little. She liked picturing the brothers as playmates. Jasper had mentioned he and Brigston weren't close, but they must have been at one time. What had changed and why? "Your mother found no fault with such behavior?"

"Boys are allowed a little more freedom than girls, but as you learned with your father, what Mother did not know she couldn't scold us for later." His conspiratorial grin made Abby's smile widen. He really was kind.

"When Jasper returns, perhaps I will ask him to teach me to swim," she said.

"I'm sure he'd be happy to oblige you at some point, but

it would probably be best to wait until after . . ." His voice trailed off, but his glance at her midsection finished his thought for him.

"The child is born?" Abby asked. There was a time when she had been painfully shy, but after making the acquaintance of Prudence Gifford, now Lady Knave, Abby had learned that if she wanted to connect with others, she couldn't hide her true self. It was a lesson that had served her well over the years, though there were some connections she could have done without.

A dark cloud settled around her at the thought, but Abby shooed it away.

"I never did ask. How long before . . ." Once again, Brigston's words drifted off, and it took a moment for Abby to deduce his meaning.

"My lying in?"

His obvious discomfort made Abby smile again. She found it amusing that such a confident man would have a difficult time speaking about her condition, however delicate it was. "The doctor said early February. He also said I should begin to feel movement soon, but I have felt nothing beyond an ever-increasing lump."

Brigston's eyes widened slightly, and his cheeks became ruddy. Her candor had definitely set him to blushing now, and she was glad to see it. Perhaps now he'd try to avoid her as she did him.

After a moment of awkwardness, he said, "Not a bad month to be born, I suppose."

"Why is that?" Abby had always thought February a dreary month—four weeks a person had to muddle through before catching glimpses of spring.

"I was born in February."

"Oh." Abby scrambled for something to say. "Well, if

it's a boy, perhaps we'll christen him after you." Merciful heavens, what had possessed her to say such a thing? Even if her child *was* a boy, Jasper wouldn't want to name him after his brother, a man he considered to be much too serious.

"If it's a girl?" Brigston asked.

"I will call her Caroline after my mother." Assuming Jasper agreed, of course. They hadn't really discussed the child, other than the fact that it existed and would be arriving after the first of the year.

"It's a beautiful name," Brigston said.

"She was a beautiful woman, or so I've been told. She died giving birth to me." Abby wondered if her candor had made him uncomfortable again, but he appeared more contemplative than anything.

"I'm sorry to hear it," he finally said.

Abby nodded and swallowed. Every time she thought ahead to the upcoming months, fears and concerns pervaded. Would she be like her mother and die giving birth to this child? Would her child die? How much pain would she have to endure before all was over and done? If they both survived the ordeal, would she be able to love her child as her father had never loved her?

Brigston must have seen the apprehension in her expression because he gently touched her arm. "Everything will be fine, Abby. Dr. Glendale is the best in the county. He will see to it that no harm will come to you or your child."

While Abby appreciated his words, she stiffened at his touch. She wasn't sure why, exactly. It was nothing more than a kind gesture from a concerned brother, but these days everything felt out of kilter. Goodness, what was wrong with her?

There was a time when Jasper's touch had caused her insides to flutter, back when they had first been introduced.

Handsome and charming, his smile had weakened her knees and warmed her belly. He'd swept into her life, showering her with attention and praise and posies and making her feel like the most desired woman in existence. She had been so taken with him. What had changed, and when had it changed?

It hadn't been instantaneous. Her attraction had simply paled. While she admired his cheerful nature and sense of adventure, Abby began to crave something deeper—the kind of connection that went beyond frivolity and playfulness. She'd wanted to marry a man to whom she could bare her soul, one who could offer her advice and comfort and make her feel as though she wasn't alone any longer.

Now, however, she didn't want to be married at all.

Perhaps in time that would change. *She and Jasper* would change. It was a hope she clung to like nothing else.

"Are you well?" Brigston's voice cut through her troubled thoughts, startling Abby.

She stiffened. "I am in perfect health, sir, all things considering."

"What I mean is, are you happy here? You seem to keep to yourself much of the time, and with Jasper gone, I . . . well, I want to be sure that you have everything you need. It can't be easy to be left alone in a new, hopefully not too strange, place with people you hardly know."

His words had a calming effect on her nerves. He seemed in earnest, as though he understood a little of her predicament and wanted to do what he could to help her. It was something a friend might have said, or at least a potential friend. What would it be like to find such a person at Oakley?

"It's good of you to ask, my lord, but you forget that I was raised by an elusive father and an indisposed great-aunt.

Long ago, I learned to find happiness in solitude." It was true enough, although the few months she'd spent with Prudence, Knave, and Sophia made her realize that she liked having friends around her more. She'd also liked the balls and parties, morning calls, and excursions to the theater and museums. But she didn't mind being on her own either. There were different kinds of happiness, she supposed.

"I only hope you can come to feel at home here," Brigston said. "Jasper has probably already told you as much, but please feel free to roam the house, curl up with a book by the fire, ask our coachman to drive you to town, or ring for a servant if you are hungry or in need of anything else. Oakley is your home now, and I'd like you to consider it as such."

Abby appreciated his thoughtfulness more than she could say. While Jasper had seen to her needs, he'd never told her she was free to explore the house or inquire about a ride in the stables. Abby had only felt at liberty to walk the grounds. But now . . . oh, how she'd dearly love to borrow a horse and go for a ride down this same stretch of beach. She'd also love to peruse the shops in town and find a modiste who could make her some new gowns to accommodate her expanding figure.

"Thank you, Brigston. I will certainly make myself more at home."

"I hope you do." He smiled briefly before turning back to his horse and adjusting the reins around the animal's neck. Before he mounted, he looked over his shoulder at her. "Would you like me to walk with you back to the house? You have come a long way."

For a moment, she was tempted to say yes, but her damp and sandy feet reminded her that she was in no condition to make the trek back to the house, at least without her boots, and she wasn't about to don her footwear in his presence.

"I'd like to stay a while longer if you don't mind."

He nodded before swinging up on his horse. "I shall see you at dinner then. Enjoy the serenity. That boulder there is a good place to rinse and dry your feet before putting your stockings and boots back on."

She chuckled. "I shall put it to good use then."

He galloped away, but rather than feel relief that he'd finally gone, loneliness encased her. She found herself yearning for her husband's companionship once more, then frowned when she realized it was all she yearned for. How strange it was not to understand one's own emotions. Jasper was a good man. A kind man. A handsome man. Why could she not *feel* something for him?

Abby pressed her lips together, thinking back to those dark days and the decision she'd made out of fear. As she'd stood at the anvil in that cluttered, dingy blacksmith's shop and spoke words she couldn't remember any longer, she'd promised herself that she would strive to care for Lord Jasper Campbell with every ounce of love she possessed. But now she struggled to do even that for him.

What sort of heartless wretch was she?

The moment tears threatened to spill, Abby straight-ened her shoulders and lifted her chin, reaffirming her resolve. She would not give up. *She would not.* Jasper still held a piece of her heart, even if it was a tiny piece. How could he not after what he'd done for her? She owed him her life and whatever tender feelings she could give. She would be a loyal wife to him, she would focus on the good in him, and she would grow to love him with *all* her heart. She was Lady Jasper Campbell now, and from this point forward, she would do whatever it took to become that person.

ABBY HAD ONLY just entered the house when Lady Brigston's resonant voice called to her from the drawing room. After a brief hesitation, Abby forced her feet to carry her to the threshold, where she dipped into a quick curtsy.

"Good afternoon, my lady."

"I had cook set aside a tray for you since you missed luncheon. I assumed you would be hungry."

Only seconds before Abby had been ravenous, but as soon as she'd heard Lady Brigston's voice, her stomach became a ball of nerves. She wasn't sure she could eat any longer, especially not here, with her mother-in-law's critical eye observing her every move. Would she ever feel at ease around this woman?

Lady Brigston was the epitome of well-bred elegance and made Abby keenly aware of her own deficiencies. The woman spoke in cultured tones, always said the right thing, did the right thing, and had the right upbringing. Abby doubted she'd ever slouched even for a moment, and she was certain Lady Brigston had never removed her stockings to wade through the cool waters of the Solent.

How different she was from her two sons. How different her sons were from each other.

"Thank you, my lady," Abby said. "Would you mind if I took the tray up to my room?"

"Actually, I was hoping to speak with you."

Dread mixed with nerves didn't help her appetite, but Abby took a seat and began nibbling at a slice of bread. She would have to get used to her mother-in-law eventually. Now was as good a time as any to start.

"Abby, we have a tradition in our parish the vicar's wife began years ago. For every child that is born, the dear woman makes a christening gown as a gift for the mother. Last week, however, she fell ill and cannot make the promised gowns for a mother of twins, who are due to arrive any day. The vicar visited only this morning to ask if I would make them in her stead, and I thought—or rather hoped—that you'd be willing to help me with the task. I could use an extra pair of hands, and . . . Are you handy with the needle, by chance?"

Lady Brigston raised her brow skeptically, no doubt thinking her daughter-in-law was undoubtedly more handy with a whip than a needle. It rankled a bit. Abby was not wholly unrefined.

She swallowed the mushy bread in her mouth and tried to smile. "I'm sure my talents won't surpass your own, but I can sew a neat stitch when necessary. It will be my pleasure to help."

"Wonderful." Lady Brigston looked both pleased and relieved. "I have everything cut out and ready to go. You can sew the pieces of one together while I work on the embroidery of the other." In other words, Lady Brigston would trust Abby to sew basic stitches, but the intricacies of embroidery should be left to the more adept of the two.

Abby examined the neatly folded piles of white muslin on the sofa between them, thinking she hadn't spent all of her time frolicking with the cows. Great-aunt Josephine had been an exacting teacher once upon the time, especially when it came to needlepoint. Abby had learned at the hand of a master, and when she'd discovered two trunks in the attic, filled with old gowns of her mother's, Abby had put that skill to use, remaking them into afternoon dresses, morning gowns, riding habits, and even a ball gown or two. How she'd loved wearing fabric that had once been worn by her mother. It made her feel as though she hadn't lost everything.

She pulled a needle from the cushion, making sure the

tip was sharp and the eye not too large, before threading it. Then she picked up a pile of muslin, sorted through the pieces, and began sewing two seams together. As expected, Lady Brigston cast covert glances her way, but in this one thing, Abby was confident she wouldn't disappoint.

"Have you had any word from Jasper?" her mother-in-law asked.

"I received a note yesterday. He said the hunt will begin soon but did not say when he would return."

She nodded. "I'm certain he will return soon. My son knows his duty."

Abby bit her lip. Apparently, her husband would return out of duty and not because he missed or desired the company of his wife. In the past, when she'd entertained dreams of marriage, this was nothing like what she'd imagined.

At least Jasper would *say* he had missed her even if he did not mean it. In all their time together, he'd only ever been complimentary towards her, sometimes a little too complimentary. Abby didn't know if she should be happy or frustrated by that aspect of his character. While she appreciated his endless optimism and gallantry, she never knew what to believe and what to discard. Which was better, a man who spoke the absolute truth, even if it was hurtful at times, or a man who turned everything into flowery speeches?

"I shall look forward to seeing him soon then," said Abby. She glanced up from her stitching, wondering about the woman before her. Had Lady Brigston loved her late husband? Did she miss him? What sort of marriage had they experienced?

"What was Jasper's father like?" she blurted. "Will you tell me something about him, if it's not too painful that is?"

47

Abby would have worried she'd overstepped, but a slight smile touched Lady Brigston's lips, softening the lines around her eyes and mouth. "Adam was everything I was not. Vivacious, endearing, and so very tall. He looked and behaved much like Jasper in many respects, though as he aged, he became more steady, if you can understand what I mean."

Abby thought she understood. Indeed, added steadiness sounded wonderful to her. Perhaps in time, she would be able to say the same of Jasper.

"He was not a typical father who left the rearing of his boys to a nursemaid. From the time they could walk, Adam taught them to fish, climb trees, ride, and even swim. When they were old enough, he bought them rifles, and they learned to hunt. The three of them were very close, and once they left for school, Adam would eagerly await their return during the breaks. He used to drive me mad, pacing about, glancing out the window every few seconds, but the moment he spotted the carriage coming around the bend, his grin warmed my heart."

She set her embroidery on her lap, and a look of sadness crossed her features. "One particular break, Jasper opted not to return home, choosing instead to spend the time at a friend's estate. Gradually, that became the norm with him. Oxford changed him. His friends changed him. Life changed him. Adam would never admit it, but it broke his heart, and after he passed on, Brigston began to change as well. Where Jasper became increasingly frivolous, Brigston became more solemn."

Lady Brigston's eyes shown bright with unshed tears as she looked at Abby. "I cannot tell you how pleased I am that Jasper has found you. I may seem disapproving at times, but you have brought my son home. Although he has gone away for a short while, I'm hopeful that you and your unborn child will become the steadying influence he needs in his life." She smiled at Abby. "I have already told the vicar's wife that *I* will be making the christening gown for my grandchild."

Abby didn't know how to feel or respond. While her mother-in-law's sincerity warmed her soul, she feared Lady Brigston would be disappointed. Her? A steadying influence on Jasper? Abby might have laughed at the idea if the circumstances were at all laughable. The only reason Jasper had come home, as Lady Brigston put it, was because Abby discovered she was increasing. She was also certain her husband considered her to be more of an impediment than a blessing.

I will change that, she vowed silently to herself.

As soon as Jasper returned, she'd do whatever it took to cherish and win the heart of her husband. Perhaps with both women hoping and praying, a positive transformation would come about. Miracles were not unheard of, after all.

"You've painted such a lovely picture of your husband and sons," said Abby. "Do you think Jasper will teach this little one how to fish, swim, climb trees, and hunt?"

"I do," said Lady Brigston with a twinkle in her eyes. "And you will teach him or her how to order cows about."

Abby chuckled, and her mother-in-law did as well. For the first time since meeting the woman, Abby felt a glimmer of hope. Even if Jasper never became the sort of husband or father they both wished him to be, perhaps Lady Brigston would become something more than an austere and disapproving mother-in-law. Perhaps she could become a mother.

FIVE

"ABBY, THIS IS remarkable." Lady Brigston inspected the embroidery Abby had stayed up half the night finishing. She'd wanted to gain her mother-in-law's approval in some way, so she had taken one of the christening gowns to bed with her and had burned through an entire candle before she'd been satisfied enough to set it aside and get some rest. That morning, she'd looked it over again with a pleased smile. The intricate line of ivy and flowers she'd sewn above the waistline was some of her best work. She'd sent up a silent prayer that Lady Brigston would agree and took the finished gown with her to the breakfast parlor.

"Each side of the design appears to be an exact replica of the other. However did you do it?" Warm brown eyes peered across the table at Abby, and she had to fight the urge not to blush.

"I draw my designs on paper with ink, lay the fabric over top, and trace them using a sharpened pencil. It isn't perfect, but I'm pleased with how it turned out. I hope you don't mind that I took the liberty of embroidering this dress without your consent."

"Why would I mind when it is superior to mine? I only worry the mother will want the twins to look the same." Her brow furrowed as she held the gown up for inspection once more. "They will be mostly the same, I suppose. Only the embroidery is different. Do you think she will care?"

"If it were me, I would want some distinguishing feature to help me tell them apart."

Lady Brigston nodded thoughtfully. "I hadn't considered that." She carefully folded the fabric and placed it on the table at her side. "That settles it then. I shall finish the other one this afternoon, and we'll deliver them on the morrow. I can't thank you enough for your help, Abby. You have proven yourself to be quite the seamstress. I am impressed."

"I'm glad to have at least one redeeming quality." Abby smiled, hoping Lady Brigston would take her teasing in stride.

"You have already proven to have more than one, my dear. You can draw as well."

Abby grimaced and shook her head. "Not unless you call forgery a talent. I stole the ivy design from one of the pillows in my room."

Lady Brigston chuckled. "Then you are a marvelous forger."

From the corner of her eye, Abby saw Brigston enter the room. She brightened, ready to turn her smile on him until she noticed his ashen face.

He quickly dismissed the few servants in the room before closing the door, his body trembling as he leaned against it for support.

Lady Brigston stood and faced him. "What is it, Morgan?"

He closed his eyes briefly, and a tear rolled down his cheek. Good heavens, something terrible must have happened. Abby froze, wondering if she should leave. Was this a private family matter? Had Brigston even noticed her?

"Tell me this instant," demanded his mother, her voice shaky but stern.

"A messenger just arrived from Barlow. He rode all night to inform us that . . ." Brigston's voice became ragged, and he looked at Abby. "Jasper has met with an accident. He's . . . he's gone."

Gone? Abby thought. *As in . . . gone?*

No.

It suddenly felt as though all the air left the room. Abby leaned over the table, gulping in air, her thoughts frenzied and frantic.

Gone.

It couldn't be. It just . . . *couldn't*. Not now, not when she had determined to change, to be better. Surely God wouldn't deprive her of that opportunity.

"What do you mean, gone?" demanded Lady Brigston in a shaky voice. The question was almost a challenge, daring her son to give her an answer she could accept.

"He's dead, Mother."

Lady Brigston's hands covered her mouth as she shook her head. "No," came her whispered plea. "No."

Abby felt the room tilt and spin. She closed her eyes against the pain of loss, disappointment, and strangled hopes. Jasper was dead—the man who'd always seemed impervious to everything, who could find something to laugh about even in the most dire of circumstances, the man who had willingly sacrificed his freedom to protect hers.

Her chest clenched in anguish. This was all so wrong. So very, very wrong.

Brigston went to his mother, enfolding her in his arms as he searched Abby's gaze. Lady Brigston's strength must have finally given way because she clung to her son and began to sob into his shoulder. The sound wrenched at Abby's heart, tearing it apart even more.

She stared at the mother and son as one might from the outside, looking in. Sounds and thoughts collided in her head, thundering through it like a herd of cattle on the run. When it reached the point she couldn't handle it any longer, Abby rushed to the door and threw it open, ignoring Brigston when he called out to her. She ran to her bedchamber, slammed and bolted the door, then crumbled to the floor in a wretched heap, clinging to her knees and burying her head in her skirts.

Why did good and honorable people have to die while deplorable people lived and breathed and went about their deplorable lives? God was supposed to be good and just, but where was the justice in this? Where was the mercy? Where was the love?

I could have loved him the way he deserved to be loved. I could have been a good wife. I could have made him more steady.

Jasper did not deserve this fate. His family didn't deserve to suffer the consequences.

Abby lifted her tear-strewn cheeks to the ceiling. *Why, God, why? Why didn't you take me instead?*

Even as she thought it, Abby felt a fluttering in her abdomen. She slowly dropped her hand to her belly, wishing with all her heart that she could have another go at this past year. If she could, she would be wiser and less self-absorbed. She would make different choices, accept the responsibilities for those choices, and seize control of her life instead of turning it over to others.

If only such a thing were possible, Jasper would still be alive.

A hollow, oppressive feeling weighed down on her, eating up the last of her strength. Abby lay down on the cold, marble floor and curled into a ball.

THE DAYS DRAGGED by in a blur of grays. Thunder shook the gloomy skies, and for the first time in weeks, rain poured down upon Oakley Grange, beating against the roof and slamming into the windows. An undertaker had been engaged to handle all funeral preparations, but Lady Brigston insisted that she and Abby would wash and dress Jasper's body.

They worked mostly in silence, saying only what needed to be said. There seemed to be no tears left to cry—only grim countenances as they watched their son and husband's body being laid out on a table in a room shrouded in black silk. Friends and neighbors came to pay their respects, speaking in quiet, cheerless voices, but it all sounded loud to Abby.

It wasn't the thing for women to attend the burial services, so Abby watched from her bedchamber window. A small chapel sat on a small rise in the distance. It was no longer used for meetings, but generations of Campbells had been buried in that churchyard, so the local clergyman had agreed to officiate. Though it was too far away to make out details, Abby could see a cluster of men gathered around the gravesite. She couldn't pry her eyes away as they lowered the coffin into the ground and covered it with layer after layer of earth.

After a time, the solemn group returned to the house, all except one, that is. Abby would recognize his straight back and sturdy frame anywhere. Brigston stood next to the grave, holding his hat in his hands with his head bowed. How lonely and small he appeared on that rise.

Abby swallowed against what had become a constant lump in her throat and turned away from the scene. Tonight she'd be expected to dine with those who had come to mourn. She'd be expected to accept their condolences and thank them for coming.

She dreaded it.

How could she look the others in the eye? How could she pretend her pain was more or equal to theirs when they'd known Jasper longer and better than she had? Their memories of him dated back to his school days, childhood, and birth. Abby had only been granted a few months with him, and during that time, he'd masked his true self. She knew that his favorite food was venison, his favorite color was blue, and his favorite breed of dog was a bloodhound, but she hadn't uncovered anything deeper than that. Jasper had let people see what he wanted them to see, nothing more.

Now here she was, the bereaved widow—the person who should be suffering the most.

Abby felt like a fraud. Although she'd cared for Jasper, she missed what they might have become more than what they'd had. Her name might be Lady Jasper Campbell, but she didn't belong to this family or Jasper's circle of friends, and she certainly didn't deserve to mourn as one of the chiefs among them.

For a brief moment, she considered crying off from dinner. They would understand. How could they not? But that would be the cowardly thing to do, and if there was one thing Abby had learned over the past few months, cowardice only worsened matters. She would go to that dinner, she would graciously thank all those who had come, and in the coming days, she would tell the Dowager Lady Brigston and her eldest son what she should have told them from the beginning.

She owed them that much.

SIX

MORGAN RUBBED HIS dry and tired eyes, blinking at the documents his solicitor had recently delivered. As much as he didn't want to deal with any of this right now, Jasper had left his finances in a muddle, and there were certain matters that needed to be dealt with straightaway, especially when it came to Abby.

"My lord," said his solicitor quietly, "you ought to think this through before making any rash decisions."

Morgan firmed his jaw. "This is not a rash decision. My brother amassed most of those debts prior to his marriage, and Lady Jasper should not be made to pay for them."

"It is not Lady Jasper's money any longer, my lord. No marriage settlements were made or signed. Her entire portion became your brother's as soon as they married, and that sum should now be used to pay for his debts. If there is anything left, we can settle it on the child."

"You know as well as I that there won't be anything left." Morgan sounded as frustrated as he felt. "It isn't right to leave Abby with nothing simply because *she* behaved rashly. I'll not stand by and allow that to happen."

"But, sir—"

"Enough, Mr. Kline," Morgan said firmly. "You may go

now. Please send word when the papers are ready to be signed."

"Yes, my lord." The deep grooves around the solicitor's eyes and mouth made his displeasure clear. Mr. Kline had served Morgan's family for nearly forty years. He was intelligent, hard-working, and trustworthy, but he managed money using his mind and not his heart. Normally that was a good thing, but in this situation, compassion was required.

Not five minutes after the solicitor had gone, a quiet knock sounded on the door.

"Enter." Morgan threaded his fingers together over the documents and waited.

Abby took a step inside the room, looking ghostly against the stark black of her mourning dress. The morbid color did not suit her at all, nor did the dark circles under her eyes. If it wasn't for the golden highlights in her hair, she'd look like death itself.

"Smithson said you wished to speak with me." She curtsied, appearing as though she'd lost some weight when she should be gaining it. Her appearance only reaffirmed Morgan's resolve to put an end to some of her troubles.

He gestured to the chair opposite him. "Please have a seat. There are some things we need to discuss about your financial situation. I realize this is not a conversation either of us wants to have right now, but it cannot be helped."

Abby nodded and did as he asked, but before he could decide where to begin, she blurted, "You needn't explain the sorry facts to me, Brigston. I am well aware of the disadvantages of elopement and the precarious position of my affairs."

Morgan ran the quill's feather through his fingers. "Precarious is putting it mildly. You've been left with nothing, Abby."

She drew in a shuddering breath but still met his gaze squarely. "Do not think I expect you to provide for me. As soon as I can make the arrangements, I will be leaving."

Morgan didn't know what he'd been expecting her to say, but not that. He'd assumed she'd remain at least until the babe was born if not longer. They were her family now. Where would she go? To her absentee father's home? Back to Lord and Lady Knave?

"You wish to leave?"

"Wish it or not, I can't remain. I don't belong here."

Morgan couldn't fathom how she'd arrived at that conclusion. "We are brother and sister, Abby. You are carrying my nephew and my mother's grandchild. You belong at Oakley Grange as much as I do."

Abby shook her head, her hands running up and down her skirts in a nervous fashion. "You don't understand."

"Pray, enlighten me."

She pressed her lips together and blinked rapidly. When she glanced towards the window, Morgan caught the sheen of unshed tears sparkling in her lovely, blue eyes. She was crying? Why? He'd said nothing offensive or unkind, had he? On the contrary, he'd honored her by calling her family. Deuce take it, she *was* family.

Morgan leaned back in his chair. "Abby, you are under no obligation to stay. If you'd prefer to go elsewhere, Mother and I will support you in any way that we can. But, like it or not, you *are* family now, and—"

"The child I am carrying is not Jasper's." The words came out in a tumbled, anguished rush.

For a moment, Morgan thought he'd heard wrong, but the sheen in her eyes, the shame and misery in her expression, and her clammy, fidgeting hands all testified that he had not. He stared at her in disbelief.

"If not Jasper's, then whose?"

She shook her head, her eyes dropping to her hands. Her lips trembled before she pressed them together in a tight line.

Morgan didn't want to believe her. He might have found several reasons not to if her admission had not shed some light on other things. The short courtship, the elopement, the lack of joy in her features at the wedding ball. The truth of it churned his stomach.

Abby was carrying someone else's child.

"Did Jasper know?"

"Yes."

Another shock—one Morgan found more difficult to believe. Jasper would never knowingly marry a ruined woman. He may have enjoyed living life recklessly, but he had always been careful not to cross a line that would cast lasting pallor on his high standing in society. He'd valued his reputation too much—or at least that's what Morgan had always assumed. But if that had truly been the case, why had he eloped? Had Jasper fancied himself so in love with Abby it made him blind? Had the truth not come to light until after they'd married? Had *she* been the one to suggest Gretna Green?

No, he couldn't believe that either. Jasper wouldn't have been lured into the parson's trap so easily, even by a woman with an alluring figure and pretty blue eyes. Besides, if Abby was capable of such deception, she wouldn't be revealing all this now.

There had to be a better explanation.

Perhaps Jasper's debts had caught up with him, and they'd struck a bargain. If she gave him her extensive dowry, he would save her from ruin.

It was the only thing that made sense, yet it didn't

explain everything. Why would Jasper give up his cherished bachelorhood when he could have come to Morgan for help? He had never been shy about asking his brother for money before.

Then there was Abby, a woman who'd seemed kind and good and *virtuous*.

Devil take it. Have I been so blind?

"Whose child is it?" he demanded again, his voice hard and cold.

Abby didn't crumble or fall into weeping as Morgan expected she might. Instead, she seemed to pull herself together and stiffen her shoulders. "His name does not matter, but I would like to explain if you are willing to hear me out. I'll understand if you'd rather I leave now."

Not matter? Morgan wanted to shout. *How could the man's identity not matter? He's the father of your child!*

He fought to remain calm, but he had never felt more deceived or wronged by his own family. All this time, his brother had known and not bothered to enlighten anyone. Did their mother know as well?

Surely Jasper would have told Morgan before their mother.

Surely.

He clenched his jaw and stared at Abby. Part of him wished he could send her packing while another part craved answers to his many questions. Why was she telling him this now? Was there a reason she married Jasper and not the man responsible? Who was she protecting, and why was she protecting him?

How did she still appear so blasted innocent when she was anything but?

Fighting to control his rising ire, Morgan leaned back in his chair and folded his arms. "I would like the rest of the story, *my lady*."

She winced at the condemning way he'd used her title, as well she should. She wasn't deserving of it. To her credit, she did not tear up again. Perhaps she knew it would only irritate him further.

"It's a long story," she said quietly.

"I have all the time in the world."

She nodded and drew in a deep breath, directing her gaze out the window beyond him. "About a year ago I became friends with our steward's nephew. I was lonely, and he was kind to me. At one point, I even fancied myself in love with him and didn't discourage a kiss every now and again. But when he tried to do more than kiss me, I realized I was headed down a foolish and dangerous path, so I told him we couldn't remain friends any longer. He attempted to convince me otherwise, but in time he realized the futility of his arguments and came around.

"I left for London, thinking that would be the end of it. But I was wrong. He began writing to me every week. At first, his notes were harmless enough—news about the estate, anecdotes that would have made me laugh at one point, and so on. When I didn't respond, his letters became more frequent and insistent. He said he couldn't rid his mind of me, and he wanted to see me again. It frightened me enough that I finally wrote to him, asking him not to write anymore. I even said that I was courting your brother and would likely be betrothed by the season's end, even though we had only just met. I never expected Jasper to come up to scratch, of course. I only hoped the lie would convince the other man to finally leave me be. It seemed to do the trick, at least for a short while."

Her eyes became haunted and sad. Morgan realized he was clutching the arms of his chair, anxious to hear more even though he already had a good idea of how the story would unfold. It sickened him.

"The beginning of May," she continued, "I received another note from him, begging me to meet him. He said he'd come to London for a meeting, and he wanted to apologize and say goodbye in person. Though I had no desire to see him again, I agreed because I wanted to be free of him so badly. We arranged to meet at Vauxhall Gardens the following Friday, when I would be there with Lord Jasper and a large party. I managed to sneak away from the group and found Will in a remote section of the gardens. We were such good friends at one point. I didn't imagine him capable of . . ."

She closed her eyes and shook her head shamefully. "He hadn't come to apologize at all. He was so angry. He accused me of giving him false hope and playing with his affections. Said he'd come to collect what was owed to him. When he grabbed me, I screamed, but my cries must have been swallowed up in the sounds of the orchestra. No one came. I tried to fight and kick my way free, but Will was too strong or I was too weak."

Her eyes began to gloss over once more, but Morgan felt no irritation this time, only pity and sorrow and loathing for a man who would behave in such a heinous manner.

"Once he'd enacted his revenge, he left me on the ground in a torn and wretched state. I crawled to a shadowed corner and huddled there for a long while. At some point, the fireworks began. I couldn't see them, but they were so loud. I wanted to flee, but the only direction I knew was the way I'd come, and I wasn't about to go there, nor was I in any condition to wander. Not long after, I heard Jasper shouting my name. The moment he saw me, I was certain he'd turn away from me in disgust, but he didn't. He heard my sobs, ascertained what had happened, and carried me away from that wretched scene. The fireworks were still in progress so we were able to leave and locate a hackney with ease. During the ride back to the townhouse, Jasper asked me to run away with him. He said we could drive to Gretna Green that very night with no one the wiser. That he'd love nothing more than to take me as his wife. I could scarce believe it."

She exhaled slowly and swallowed before continuing. "In my weakened and miserable state, I agreed, and before I could rethink the decision, we were on our way to Gretna Green."

She wiped a tear from her cheek and tried to smile. "I still don't know why Jasper did what he did or why I let him. It was madness. I keep thinking that if I had only been stronger or wiser or less selfish, we wouldn't have married and he'd still be alive. But he isn't, and nothing I can do or say will change that."

Tears spilled freely from her eyes as she lifted them to his. "Why couldn't it have been me and not him? I had nothing to lose and he had everything."

Morgan's heart wrenched. It was no wonder Jasper wanted to rescue her. One look at those tear-stained cheeks and bright blue eyes and any man would feel the pull to do the same, although few men would have offered their protection in the way Jasper had. The fact alone was nothing short of astounding.

"It's not your fault he died, Abby. I know my brother well. He could never say no to a hunting party."

She negated him with a shake of her head. "He had already written his refusal, insisting his rightful place was at my side and that's where he would remain. It was me who told him to go. I could see how much he yearned for it, how restless he was becoming here, so I encouraged him to accept, thinking I was doing him a kindness."

"You *were* doing him a kindness, and he still made the choice to go. His accident was not your fault any more than it was mine or his friends. As morbid as it sounds, death is part of life. It'll come to all of us at one point or another, and there is nothing we can do to stop that. It's simply harder to bear when it happens before we think it should."

Morgan hoped she found some comfort in his words, or at least forgave him for the harsh way he'd reacted to her news. Whatever ire he still felt was now directed at the man who'd done this to her, if he could be called a man at all. Had Jasper done anything to seek recompense? Had he called the perpetrator out? Beat him within an inch of his life? At the very least, turned him over to a Bow Street Runner, not that justice would have been served. Acts of such savagery rarely saw justice. The cur need only say that Abby encouraged him, and the law would look the other way—or worse, force Abby to marry him.

Morgan clenched the arms of his chair as his stomach roiled at the thought. A man like that did not deserve a woman like Abby. He deserved to be hung from the gallows.

"When I discovered I was increasing," Abby continued, "Jasper said he would claim the child as his own and never breathe a word to anyone about his or her true parentage. I know I have no right to ask the same of you, but for the sake of the child, it is my hope that you and Lady Brigston will honor his desire and remain silent on the subject." She placed her hand over her stomach in an absentminded fashion. "The babe is innocent of any wrongdoing and should not be made to suffer for circumstances beyond his or her control. I will never ask anything more of you than that."

Although she appeared anxious, she held herself with pride. Morgan had to commend her for that *and* for her honesty. She could have kept all these sordid facts to herself, and Morgan and his mother would have been none the wiser.

"How can you be certain the child is not Jasper's?" The question wasn't one he wanted to ask, but he needed to know. If there was even a small chance it could be his brother's, Morgan could see no reason for this discussion or for revealing the truth to his mother.

Her face turned a light crimson color, and she diverted her gaze. "Jasper and I . . ." She closed her eyes and blurted, "We never consummated our marriage. He wanted to, but after what had happened, I couldn't bear to have another man touch me. I told him I needed some time, and he was good enough to give it to me." When her eyes opened again, they were wet. "I would love to believe the child could be Jasper's, but I can tell you with absolute certainty it is not."

Morgan had no idea what to say to this. He'd been so quick to condemn his brother *and* Abby, so quick to assume the worst in both of them.

How wrong he'd been.

"Why are you telling me this?" he asked.

She took a moment to answer. "I never wanted to hide it, at least not from you or your mother. But Jasper insisted that the fewer people who knew the better. He didn't see any reason to explain the situation to you, and he didn't want to trouble your mother. I respected his wishes even though I did not agree. But now that he is gone, I can no longer live with the deceit. Perhaps it is wrong to ask you and Lady Brigston to share the burden of secrecy, but whether or not you do so should be your choice to make, not mine."

"Do you still intend to keep the child?"

"Yes."

"You wouldn't consider turning it over to a parish? I'm certain there is a couple somewhere who would gladly welcome a babe into their home."

The proud look in her eyes hardened into steel. "The child may not be Jasper's, but it is mine. I never knew what it was like to have a real father or mother, my lord. I always felt as though my father blamed me for the death of my mother and couldn't abide being near me for long. It injured me deeply, and I would never want any child to feel unwanted. The only reason I would consider giving it up would be if I could not find a way to properly care for it myself. But I assure you, I *will* find a way. Children ought to be cherished, not abandoned."

"I admire your determination, Abby," Morgan said carefully. "But will the child not serve as a constant reminder of a vile act?"

Her hand moved over her midsection in a protective way. "I choose to believe that he or she will be a balm instead of an unpleasant reminder. How could anyone resent an innocent babe? I can only pray I won't feel that way because I desperately need something good to come from this. How else can I put it behind me?"

Morgan considered the woman before him with newfound respect. Instead of allowing hatred and fear to consume her, she was doing what she could to heal and move forward. He, on the other hand, wanted nothing more than to find the blackguard who did this to her and make him pay for what he'd done. No man should be allowed to force himself upon a woman and walk away unscathed.

He ran his thumb along the edge of the desk. "In that case, I will keep your secret, not that it matters much. By law, the child will be considered Jasper's regardless of how your confinement came about. You are his widow, and if you were carrying the child at the time of his passing, it is legally his. I see no reason for you to say anything about this to my mother, at least not at present."

The wariness in her eyes told him she didn't agree. "My lord, it is not right to keep this from her."

"Perhaps not, but I know my mother. She is a stickler for proprieties, and while I believe she would come to terms with it eventually, it will be difficult to bear so recently after Jasper's passing. She has already lost a husband and a son. Let us not make her lose Jasper's child as well. I know the truth. Can't that be enough for now?"

Abby furrowed her brow. "I understand your feelings, and I have no wish to cause her additional pain, but she wants to make a christening gown and who knows what else. I cannot, in good conscience, allow her to spend her time, energies, and money on a child she believes to be Jasper's own flesh and blood."

Morgan steepled his fingers under his chin and considered her words. They both presented valid arguments, but when it came to his mother, he felt strongly that now was not the time for honesty.

"I only ask that you allow her to heal a while longer and refrain from explaining at this juncture. When the time is appropriate, I will be the one to tell her. Please, Abby, you must trust me on this."

She finally nodded. "Very well. I shall leave it in your hands, so long as you promise to do so before she begins making the christening gown. I would like to write her a letter of explanation as well. You can give it to her when you feel the time is right."

It took Morgan a moment to realize why she'd feel the need to write a letter. She was still planning to leave. The thought didn't sit well with him. It had felt less lonely since she'd come to Oakley, and he was reluctant to see her go. Before Jasper's accident, his mother had begun to smile and laugh more as well. If given more time, he was certain she'd grow to care for Abby as a daughter, making the news of the child easier to bear. But if Abby left Oakley now . . .

"You're determined to leave?" he asked.

Her eyes widened, as though she hadn't expected it to be an option. Had she really thought he'd send her away once he learned the sordid details of her past? Did she think he'd hold her to blame?

"I believe it would be for the best, my lord," she finally said.

Morgan disagreed, though he kept that opinion to himself, saying instead, "It seems we are back to where we began. What is it *you* want to do, Abby? Leave or stay?"

His stomach became a mass of knots while he waited for her answer. Why, he couldn't say. Did he want her to stay because he felt duty-bound to provide for her, or was it more than that? If she were hideous to look upon or unpleasant to be around, would he still feel this way?

Probably not.

The fact of the matter was that Abby was becoming his friend. He liked being around her, he enjoyed their conversations and her sense of humor, and he was growing increasingly fond of her smile and laugh. He didn't want to lose that. He didn't want to lose her.

When she didn't answer straightaway, he felt the stirrings of hope. Perhaps all she needed was a reason to stay.

He cleared his throat. "Abby, I will not try to dissuade you, but you are Lady Jasper Campbell now, my late brother's widow. As such, you will always be welcome here." Even as he spoke the words, he cringed at how stiff and formal they sounded, like an offer made out of charity.

He quickly amended, "What I mean to say is that your presence here has been a delight. You have been a companion to my mother and a friend to me. I will miss you should you choose to leave."

She pressed her lips together, and a myriad of emotions flitted across her features. Consideration, hope, worry, anxiety, and finally a solemn determination. She was going to insist that leaving would be for the best, regardless of his or her wishes.

Before she could voice her thoughts, he quickly said, "You needn't decide right away. There is still much to be done to put your affairs in order. Feel free to take your time and think on it during the next week or two. You can give me your answer once all the papers have been signed."

She frowned. "What papers are you referring to? I have no claim on anything."

"Not now, but in a week or two, you will," said Morgan.

"But—"

He held up his hand to quiet her. "Abby, I would no more leave you penniless then I would allow this estate to fall to ruin. I intend to set you up with an annuity equal to what your jointure would have been if marriage settlements had been made. The law may not require me to do so, but my conscience does."

Morgan would never tire of seeing those lovely blue eyes grow wide. Only this time, they shone with good tears, endearing tears.

"I . . . don't know what to say," she finally said. "I don't deserve your generosity."

"It is not generosity to return to you what should have been yours to begin with, so let us say no more on the subject." He clasped his fingers in a gesture of finality.

"Thank you, Brigston," she said. "That sounds so inadequate, but I don't know how else to tell you how much your kindness, understanding, and compassion mean to me."

Her words, spoken with warmth and sincerity, stirred something within Morgan. Despite what his solicitor had cautioned him against and what his bailiff would undoubtedly say, he'd done the right thing. Jasper's debts would cost him dearly and set him back for a time, but at least he could move forward with a clear conscience.

"It is my pleasure, Abby," he said. "Now, if you'd be so kind as to ask Smithson to summon my bailiff, I'd appreciate it."

She rose to do as he bid, but before she quit the room, Morgan added, "Please think about what we discussed. I would truly be sorry to see you go."

She smiled a little before walking out the door, leaving Morgan feeling unsettled and nervous. By restoring funds to her, he'd given her the means to live in comfort independently of him and everyone else.

How strange it felt to grant her freedom while hoping she would not take it.

THE SKIES DARKENED to dusk as Morgan ascended the small rise to the churchyard's burial plot. It was a peaceful spot—the old stone chapel surrounded by buckthorn, aspen, and beech trees. Over the past few years, he'd come to his father's grave every now and again, whenever he'd had a troubling decision to make. At first, he'd come to express frustration. His father hadn't left Oakley in the best state, and Morgan had several choice words to say to his sire. But as he began to set Oakley to rights, he no longer felt the need to lecture and came instead to work through various problems. It helped, somehow.

Today, however, Morgan had come to speak to his brother.

Jasper's grave marker was tall and rectangular, with a

decorative arch across the top. The design was simple but still in good taste. Jasper probably would have chosen something more elaborate, but as soon as Morgan had set eyes on this stone, he knew it was the one. It reminded him of the old Jasper, the unassuming and authentic brother from his youth.

Morgan removed his hat, clutching it in his hands as he read the words engraved on the stone.

IN MEMORY OF A BELOVED SON,
BROTHER, HUSBAND, AND FATHER.
JASPER ARCHER CAMPBELL
3 MARCH 1792 – 17 AUGUST 1817

Morgan gave a wry smile at the word *father*. "You always did like to take credit for things not of your making. Remember when I carved an owl for that pretty farmer's daughter and left it on a stump in the meadow where we used to play? You found it first and waited for her to come along, then accepted her embrace of thanks without explaining who really carved it. I still haven't forgiven you for that."

He could almost hear Jasper's teasing answer. "I was saving you from yourself, idiot. She was only a farmer's daughter, and you were an earl."

Morgan liked remembering the Jasper from long ago—his brother, his friend, his partner in crime. How he missed that Jasper.

"Who were you, really?" Morgan asked quietly. He used to think he'd always have to look into the past to remember his brother fondly, but after Abby's confession, he had to wonder if that youthful Jasper was not as lost as Morgan had thought.

"It seems I've misjudged you, brother. You're probably looking down on me in triumph right now, so I will not pamper your vanity too much. Though you were a frivolous spendthrift until the day you died, you did well by Abby. It couldn't have been easy to sacrifice your freedom, but I commend you for doing so. As far as I'm concerned, you have earned the title of father. I only wish you could have stayed around long enough to show us the sort of father you could have become."

Morgan ran his finger across the top of the headstone. For a moment, he caught a whiff of orange that smelled like the traditional cologne his brother often wore, but then it was gone, floating away with the breeze.

He swallowed and gave the stone a final pat. "Farewell, brother. You will be missed. Rest assured that your child will be raised with every opportunity possible, and know that Abby will carry your name with grace, dignity, and spirit."

He waited a few seconds longer, then replaced his hat and walked away, feeling lighter than he had in years.

SEVEN

ABBY STOOD IN front of the window in her bedchamber and peered out at the gray skies, lush grounds, and sea in the distance. After Jasper had left for that ill-fated hunting party, she had felt something awaken inside her—a longing to make the most of her marriage and a determination to set her life to rights. When Lady Brigston began to soften towards her, it was like an extra spoonful of cream. Her hope had sparked strong and bright.

Now, all that wonderful hope had been snuffed out, leaving Abby beaten and defeated. She should have made the most of her marriage when she'd had the chance. She should have given Jasper a reason to stay instead of encouraging him to go. She should have cared for him as he had her.

Abby closed her eyes, reminding herself that it did no good to dwell on things that couldn't be altered. No matter how much she might wish for another chance, Jasper was gone.

She shivered and stepped away from the window. Her expansive bedchamber looked lovely and bright. A wooden four-poster bed gleamed against the cream walls, with peach and gold accents throughout. As soon as she'd walked into this room, it had become her haven, as had the rest of

Oakley. But now, everywhere she went, the walls, the grounds, even the sea felt like an enclosure. She no longer felt peaceful here, only a growing anxiousness to rid herself of the mournful quiet.

Abby rarely saw Brigston, and her mother-in-law kept to her bedchamber, choosing to mourn behind her thick, wooden door. Even the servants were quieter than usual, tiptoeing from room to room as though any noise would upset the precarious feeling that hovered over the house. Sometimes Abby wanted to shout loudly from the great hall, just to hear something besides the quiet.

Though she had little experience with death, Abby understood loneliness, sadness, and even loss to a certain extent. She'd learned that if she let those feelings take hold, as she had of late, her existence became dark indeed. If she didn't find some reprieve soon, she feared the oppression would swallow her up. Every day that passed, her soul wilted and withered a little more.

Abby inhaled deeply and told herself that as soon as she signed whatever papers needed signing, she would go. It was the only choice she could make.

The muffled sound of hoof beats captured her attention, and she peered out her window to see Brigston gallop away from the stables at a fast clip. She felt envious, wishing she could mount a horse and race across the countryside as well—away from this house and the morbid feelings inside her.

Why don't you?

The thought entered her mind with such vigor that she couldn't dismiss it. Although her belly bulged a little, it wasn't large enough to be a problem. She would still be able to ride without difficulty or discomfort, and Brigston *had* said she should make herself at home.

Perhaps a long, hard ride would save her from certain madness.

Yes, why not?

Abby strode to her closet to retrieve a habit, only to realize the red and gold colors staring back at her would never do for mourning apparel. For a brief moment, the disappointment weighed her down, but as she considered the black gown she wore, she had the rebellious thought that the dress would suit her as well as any habit.

Abby donned her pelisse, gloves, bonnet, and riding boots, then strode from the room before she could talk herself out of it.

In the stables, a groom attempted to dissuade her, but Abby remained firm. He finally relented, insisting she take the gentlest mare, and Abby soon found herself seated on a lovely chestnut horse, flying towards the sea.

The rush of speed and freedom whipped around her, bolstering her spirits and making her believe she *could* outrun the misery. She hadn't ridden this hard or fast in a long while, and it felt wonderful. Why hadn't she done this before now?

She rode up and down the beach, slowing the mare to a trot through a large copse of trees, then picked up the pace on the beach once more. After another lengthy canter across the shoreline, she pulled the mare to a halt and breathed in the salty air while admiring the Isle of Wight in the distance.

This was her escape—her only escape—and how desperately she'd needed it. Tomorrow, she would ride again, along with the next day and the day after that, for as long as it took to sign those papers.

When she became aware of another horse approaching from behind, she glanced back to see Brigston coming her way. This time, the sight of him didn't make her at all nervous or uncomfortable. On the contrary, she was pleased to see him. As he neared, however, he did not seem nearly as pleased to see her. In fact, he looked downright grim.

"What the devil are you doing?" he demanded.

Refusing to be cowed, Abby returned his glare with a raised brow. "Enjoying the view, obviously. Isn't the Isle of Wight inspiring? We should secure a boat and go there."

"Abby, you were racing across the beach on the back of a horse."

She chuckled lightly. "If you call that racing, you are in need of spectacles, my lord. I was merely strolling."

He rolled his eyes. "Strolling is something you do with your feet, not a horse."

Abby leaned forward and patted the animal's neck. "Her name is Sunshine, and she has the sweetest temperament."

"Sweet or not, you shouldn't—"

"Riding is a perfectly acceptable pastime for a woman," said Abby.

"Not if that woman happens to be . . . in a certain condition." He stumbled over the words, appearing uncomfortable and frustrated. Abby had to admit she rather liked watching him squirm.

"You're increasing, Abby," he said more firmly. "You shouldn't be riding at all, regardless of the pace."

"Why is that?" she challenged, ready for an argument. It felt good to speak forcefully. It felt good to speak at all.

"What if you suffered a fall? Surely the doctor has advised you against such exercise."

Abby waved the concern aside with a flip of her wrist. "Psh. He has never carried a child. How can he possibly know what I should or shouldn't be doing? I'm an adept rider, sir, and I have not increased too large as of yet."

Brigston seemed to consider her argument before

dismissing it with a shake of his head. "I'm sorry, but I must insist on this. I have already given an order to the grooms that you are not to ride again until the doctor deems you able to do so."

Nothing he said could have injured Abby more. He'd taken a mallet to her spirits, crushing them with one painful whack. Could he not see how much she needed this? Could he not trust that she knew what she was doing? If she had felt the least bit unstable or uncomfortable, she would have refrained. She would never put the well-being of her unborn child at risk.

Abby swallowed against the sudden lump in her throat as the feeling of entrapment returned with a vengeance. "I'm afraid I must leave Oakley," she blurted.

Her words sobered him instantly, and his brow furrowed. "Now?"

She hesitated. He'd made it plain he'd like her to stay, and for his sake, she wished she could acquiesce, but she needed to move forward with her life, and she didn't see how she could accomplish that while at Oakley. "I feel it's the path I should take. I find myself without purpose of late, and it makes me anxious."

He cocked his head to the side and examined her. "What are you searching for, Abby? You are to be a mother soon. Is that not purpose enough? Do you feel you can better perform that role elsewhere?"

Abby ought to have known he wouldn't be satisfied with a vague answer. Jasper probably would have, or at least he wouldn't have questioned her further. Brigston, on the other hand, wanted to understand. It was a trait she liked about him because it encouraged her to speak freely.

"I'm lonely, Brigston," she admitted. "It's become too solemn for my peace of mind. If I stay much longer, I fear I will go mad. Can you understand? Are you not also in desperate need of conversation, laughter, and something more than silence? My world has been dark for so long. I don't think I can bear anymore."

Her words seemed to sadden him. "You are anxious to leave."

She nodded. "I can't decide if it's an act of cowardice or bravery. Perhaps I should take to my bedchamber and bury my sorrow with tears, but what good will that do? Sorrow and regret will not bring my husband back. Nothing will. So why not seek joy instead? It has been too elusive of late, but I must find it soon or perish myself."

He appeared troubled, but instead of voicing his thoughts aloud, he swung down from his horse, walked to her side, and peered up at her beneath the brim of his beaver.

"Walk with me?" he asked.

She eyed his gloved fingers with both longing and trepidation. A few months ago, she didn't think she'd ever desire a man's touch again. At first, Jasper's attempts to comfort her had caused her to recoil, but after several weeks, she'd grown accustomed to him taking her hand and kissing her cheek. In time, she would have become accustomed to more, but that time had been stolen from her.

Brigston, on the other hand, had never made her recoil. Was it because he posed no threat? He was her brother, after all, and had never tried to be anything more, nor would he. Perhaps that was the reason.

She at last conceded with a nod, but as soon as his hands touched her waist, a delicious warmth traveled up her back and radiated through her limbs. His touch felt marvelous. Safe. As he set her on the ground, she breathed in the scents of leather, horse, citrus, and a tantalizing spice she couldn't describe. For a moment, Abby thought she felt her babe move within her, but she couldn't be sure if it was the babe or Brigston that made her insides flutter.

I'm healing, she thought with a start. For a moment she basked in that knowledge until the gravity of the situation made her step free from his grasp. What was wrong with her? Brigston was the last person she should feel an attraction for. He was her brother.

Abby waited while he gathered both sets of reigns in his hands, then walked beside him across the pebbly beach.

He spoke first. "It will not always be this way. We are in mourning." An underlying question of *Do you not intend to mourn my brother?* accompanied his words, or perhaps Abby only thought she detected it.

She peered off into the distance, choosing her words carefully. "I would give anything to see Jasper's smile or hear his laughter again. I feel cheated that our time together was so brief and sad that this child will never know him. It would be an easy thing to capitulate to the grief and guilt that plagues me, but Jasper would have despised being mourned in that way. He would not wish his memory to be tucked away in some dark recess because we find it too painful to speak of him. He would want to be the center of our conversations, the subject of stories and recollections. He'd want us to relive his life over and over again, laughing at his antics and remembering the good and cheerful person he was. This melancholy that abounds—it doesn't feel right to me."

Brigston nodded slowly, his brow furrowed in thought. After a minute or two, he said, "I think you'd find that many people share your feelings, but it is easier said than done, is it not? There is so much sorrow that accompanies loss. I fear mother cannot see the sun through the clouds, at least not yet. It's hard to speak of Jasper when doing so brings more pain than laughter."

Abby felt instantly humbled. He was right, of course. Who was she to tell him and his mother how to mourn? Who was she to have an opinion on anything? "Forgive my impertinence, Brigston. I cannot comprehend the extent of your mother's suffering—or yours, for that matter. I didn't know Jasper as well as you and have no idea what it must feel like to lose a child or a sibling, nor do I wish to know. Perhaps that makes me unfeeling."

"You have nothing to apologize for, Abby. I have always appreciated your honesty and hope you will continue to be direct with me. I also believe you knew Jasper better than you think. He loathed melancholy and would prefer to be at the heart of our conversations. Perhaps it would do us good to speak of him more."

Abby smiled a little, grateful he didn't dismiss her feelings outright. "When we were traveling to Gretna, I was lost to a darkness of my own making, and it was Jasper who helped me see light again. He tried various antics to encourage a smile, and when nothing worked, he finally took me by the hand and said, 'You're only as happy as you believe you can be, Abby. Hope comes from looking ahead, not behind.'

"I told him that looking ahead only caused me to worry, to which he replied, 'Then you must choose what to worry about. In my case, I'm concerned only about the weather during a hunt or a race. Rain is my greatest nemesis. But it is not raining now, is it? I think that gives us more than enough reason to hope.'"

Brigston chuckled. "That sounds like Jasper and doesn't at the same time. He was never one for serious reflection."

"Perhaps he just wanted people to think that," Abby said, smiling at the memory. It was one of the few times when Jasper's words had comforted her, one of the times she'd actually felt hope that something good could come from the bad.

Once they had stated their vows, however, Jasper buried himself behind flippancy once more, remarking on the dusty state of his chaise and how unfit it was for his bride, the esteemed Lady Jasper. From that point on, he never called her anything else. He probably wanted her to know that he would always think of her as a lady despite what happened to her, but the title made her feel like a charlatan. She would have liked it more had he called her *my darling, my dear,* or simply *Abby.*

"I like how you remember Jasper." Brigston's voice broke through her reverie. "My more recent memories of him are less rosy."

Abby might have asked him to explain, but something in his tone made her swallow the question. "There is good and bad in us all, isn't there. When it comes to Jasper, I cannot tell you how much was good and how much was not. He often hid his true self from me."

Brigston nodded. "From me as well. I could never understand why. He didn't used to."

"Perhaps he feared showing weakness."

"I don't know," said Brigston. "He seemed to enjoy making sport of his failings."

"Yes, but making sport of one's failings is different than allowing oneself to be vulnerable. It's an easy thing to joke about one's inability to distinguish a Michelangelo from a Donatello but more difficult to admit an insecurity or fear."

"You seem to have no trouble doing so," noted Brigston with a teasing lilt to his voice.

She smiled even though she didn't deserve the praise, if indeed it *was* praise. "I did not share everything with him. We are both guilty on that score."

His expression became suspect. "I find that hard to believe. You have always seemed very open to me."

"Yes, well . . ." Abby bit her lip to keep her thoughts from stumbling out as they often did with him. What would he say if he could hear them? *You're different than your brother. I find it easier to speak with you than I did with him. Even though I haven't known you long, I feel a deeper connection to you.*

She could never speak openly about that.

"Well . . . ?" he prodded.

"There is still much you do not know about me, my lord—much Jasper did not know about me as well."

To her surprise, he smiled. "Never say you enjoy mingling with sheep as well as cows."

It felt good to chuckle about something, even if that something was livestock. "Chickens, too, though they don't mind nearly as well."

Brigston laughed, then halted her progress with a hand on her arm. Even through her gown, she could feel the warmth of his touch. It made her skin tingle. "I suppose there is much I do not know about you, but that's only because we haven't been acquainted for long. Why not stay a bit longer so I can say there is only *a little* I do not know about you?"

She stared into his blue-gray eyes, feeling mesmerized. How she yearned to say she *would* stay, especially if it meant more afternoons spent like this.

But did she truly want that? Only minutes ago, she'd been ready to flee and put as much distance between her and Oakley as possible.

Abby blinked and looked away, taking a deep breath to calm her skittish heart. In a small voice she said, "I must go as soon as I am able, my lord."

Silence met her words. When it stretched on for a while, she looked back at him and was disheartened to see sadness in his expression. It weakened her resolve. "I'll return to visit if you and your mother would wish it."

"Of course we'd wish it." He tucked her hand into the crook of his elbow and began walking once more, pointing at a grove of trees in the distance. "When we were lads, Jasper decided we should build a tree fort in one of those trees so we could keep a lookout for pirates. I thought it a great plan, so we scrounged up some nails and a hammer, pried some boards from an old shed, cut them down, and nailed them into an unlucky ash tree. They made an adequate ladder, but as we climbed higher, we realized we didn't have enough wood to build a platform. So we decided to scavenge more from the chicken coop, thinking the large birds couldn't fit through the narrow openings. We were wrong, of course, and I'm sure you can imagine the chaos that ensued."

The image of two boys chasing chickens through the yard made Abby grin. How she wished she'd known the Campbell boys back then. They would have made wonderful chums.

"If Jasper were here today, he'd insist that it had been my idea to filch the wood from the coop, even though it had been his. In the end, though, it really didn't matter. We both lost dinner on account of it, though Mother brought us some food after our nurse had retired for the evening. She had a soft spot for us boys."

"I can well imagine," said Abby. It felt good to speak of Jasper in this way, to smile and laugh and learn something more about her late husband. *This*, she thought, *is how people should be mourned.*

Her father never spoke to Abby about her mother. Whenever she'd pressed him for any information, he'd find a way to quiet her many questions, either by leaving the room or redirecting the conversation. It broke Abby's heart.

She'd decided long ago that people shouldn't be forgotten. Their lives should be celebrated, their stories told, and their memory made to live on through family and friends.

"Will you tell me more?" she pleaded.

Brigston complied, beginning another story as they continued the stroll down the beach. She listened with rapture to the pleasing timbre of his voice and delighted in the feel of his arm beneath her hand as he further introduced the mischievous boy who had become her husband.

EIGHT

NOT FOR THE first time that morning, Morgan glanced out the study's window, hoping for a glimpse of Abby. Had she left earlier than usual? Had he somehow missed her? Was she already out and about, combing the beach on foot—or worse, horseback? He wouldn't be surprised if she'd ignored his wishes and managed to convince a groom to let her ride. Though he'd made his opinion clear, she hadn't agreed to comply.

He stood and walked to the window, peering out across the grounds. Perhaps he should take a ride down the beach to be sure. She was probably feeling lonely and restless again.

After their discussion yesterday, Morgan realized he needed to make an effort to seek her out. He tried to tell himself it was only for her benefit, but deep down he knew better. Only an hour with her yesterday had brightened his day considerably. He wanted it to stay bright.

A knock interrupted his surveillance, and a petite maid bustled into the room carrying a tea tray—one he hadn't requested.

Morgan quirked a brow. "What's this?"

"Monsieur Roch asked me to bring it up, milord," she said. "I'm to tell you Lady Jasper made the scones 'erself." The maid's lips twitched into half a smile.

"Indeed?" Morgan peered down at the tray and nearly laughed out loud. The scones were flat, misshapen, and much too brown. Apparently, Abby had walked to the kitchen instead of the beach this morning.

"Monsieur Roch didn't want you thinkin' they were his doin'," added the maid.

Morgan picked up one of the scones, noticing how dense it felt compared to his cook's usually light and feathery ones.

"Lady Jasper made these?" he asked.

"Aye, milord," said the maid. "She's askin' to 'elp with dessert also."

Ah, thought Morgan, understanding dawning. That was the reason Monsieur Roch sent up a tray of inedible scones. He wanted Morgan to do something about Abby before she brought ruin upon the dessert as well.

He grinned. "Please give Lady Jasper my compliments. I'm sure I will enjoy these scones with the greatest pleasure."

"Yes, milord." She curtsied, but before she could scamper from the room, Morgan added, "You needn't return for the tray. I will bring it down once I've finished."

"Thank you, milord." The obvious relief in her tone and expression made Morgan's smile widen. She could now return to Monsieur Roch having accomplished the task he'd given her.

After the door closed, Morgan examined the scones again. More out of curiosity than hunger, he slathered jam on one and took a tentative bite. The flavor wasn't bad, or perhaps the jam simply masked it, but he had to practically gnaw on the thing before he was able to swallow it. Without a second thought, he tossed the remaining scones into the fireplace and scooped up the tray.

When he entered the kitchen, Abby's back was partially to him, so she didn't immediately see him. Her brow was furrowed in concentration as she whipped something in a bowl. She paused to lift the spoon, only to frown at the white liquid dripping from it.

"Are you certain this will thicken into a cream?" she asked.

A flash of irritation crossed Monsieur Roch's face until he spotted Morgan and seemed to think better of it. He managed a patient tone in his accented French. "It takes time, my lady."

Morgan stifled a chuckle as Abby examined another spoonful of the liquid. "I've been whipping it for several minutes, but it doesn't seem even a little thicker to me. Have I forgotten to add something?"

"No," said the cook in clipped tones.

Morgan stepped forward and leaned in close. "If your arm is tired—"

Abby jumped, and what liquid remained on the spoon splattered across Morgan's face. She spun around, her eyes growing wide with horror when she saw what she'd done.

He wiped a dab from his nose and tasted it. "A little more sugar, perhaps?"

"Brigston! I'm so dreadfully sorry." She dropped the spoon into the bowl and grabbed a rag from a nearby wash basin, dabbing it across his face.

"Not that rag!" cried the cook. "It was only just used to mop the floors."

Abby dropped it as though it had burned her, and Morgan tried not to cringe at the thought of filthy water coating his face.

Monsieur Roch retrieved a clean rag and held it out to him, appearing apologetic. He flicked another irritated glance at Abby before returning to his work.

As Morgan wiped the cream from his face, he wondered

what Abby would do or say next. Offer another fumbled apology? Make her excuses and flee? Pretend the incident never happened and return to her labors? He never knew what to expect from her.

Her face scarlet, she cleared her throat and lifted her adorably determined chin. "You are most welcome, my lord."

He raised a brow. "For what, my lady?"

"I have heard that cream does wonders for one's complexion, and it seems the rumors are correct. Your skin appears much . . . creamier."

Morgan was hard pressed not to laugh, especially when several snickers sounded throughout the room. "Is that so?"

She nodded with conviction.

"How interesting." He examined the contents of the bowl, then dipped his finger into the liquid. "I would like to see the results for myself. You don't mind, do you, my lady?" He ran his finger down her nose, not waiting for an answer. To her credit, she didn't flinch or shy away.

"Does it need to sit a while?" he asked.

"Only a second or two," came her response.

It was becoming increasingly difficult not to laugh, but Morgan was determined not to succumb before she did. He wiped off the liquid and looked closely at her nose, spying a light freckle on one side. "I do believe you are right, Lady Jasper. Your nose does appear creamier. Would you like me to apply it to the rest of your face?"

Her lips twitched. "I don't think Monsieur Roch would take kindly to us using his dessert as a facial cream."

"I gather not." Morgan eyed the cook sheepishly. "Forgive us, Monsieur. If it's all right with you, I shall steal Lady Jasper for a time. I'm hoping she will accompany me on a stroll through the gardens."

"Perfectly all right," answered the cook a bit too quickly.

Abby looked suspiciously from the cook to Morgan before taking his arm. As soon as they had exited the house, she pulled free and faced him. "Was I that much of a nuisance that you needed to save the cook from my interference?"

Morgan felt contrite. She looked hurt. "I wouldn't say nuisance."

"What would you say?"

"Perhaps hindrance?" He wished the word back the moment her mouth dropped into a frown. Admittedly, it wasn't much better. "Abby, you must understand that Monsieur Roch is a busy man, and . . . well . . ." How could he possibly put it nicely?

"I was getting in his way," she finished for him, then sighed. "I'm sorry, Brigston. It wasn't my intent to hinder."

She appeared so disheartened. Morgan wanted to pull her into an embrace, if only to show her that he enjoyed her company even if the kitchen staff did not.

Instead, he asked gently, "What *was* your intent?"

She threw up her hands in frustration. "I don't know. I suppose I wanted to know the servants better? That sounds ludicrous, I know, but when I was a young girl, our cook and maids became very dear to me. Whenever I was feeling especially lonely, I would go to the kitchen, and Mrs. Wood would make me scones and preserves. She would ask after me and listen to my stories and concerns. In a way, she became the mother I never had. I miss that connection."

"And you thought Monsieur Roch could be such a person?"

She blushed, then smiled ruefully. "Let's just say that I hoped he'd be a mite friendlier. I should have known I'd only get in the way."

Morgan held out his arm, hoping she'd accept it and walk with him. "I'm afraid you'll have to content yourself with my company for now."

"But that's my point," she said. "I don't want you to feel obligated to entertain me. You are busy with the estate, and—"

"Abby." He gently took her hand and tucked it through is arm, liking how well she seemed to fit beside him. "Spending time with you is not an obligation. It is a pleasure."

She snorted. "That's doing it a bit too brown, my lord."

"Not at all. Now, where shall we walk today? To the east? The west? The beach?" When she appeared ready to argue, he added firmly, "I am asking as your friend, Abby."

She considered him a long moment before nodding hesitantly. "I would love to see the poor tree you and Jasper defiled in your attempt to build a tree fort. Will you show it to me?"

How she made him smile. He would happily show her that and anything else she wanted to see. "Very well, but if I ever catch you trying to climb the rickety ladder, assuming it's still there, I shall turn you over my knee."

She pulled her hand free, took a step back, and arched her brow at him. "Aren't you domineering? First you order me off a horse and now threaten to spank me? Do you see me as an impertinent child, my lord? Because I assure you, I am not." She grinned impishly and strode forward, saying over her shoulder, "At least not a child."

Brigston chuckled, admiring the lovely figure she made as she walked ahead. Her straight back, swinging hips, and golden hair shining in the sunlight. A few tendrils had escaped the simple knot and blew slightly in the breeze, and beneath her swishing black skirts, he caught a glimpse of a trim ankle.

No, you are most definitely not a child, he thought.

THE EVENING AT dinner, Morgan's mother joined him and Abby in the dining room. She looked dreadful. The black of her gown matched the dark circles under her eyes, and her severe chignon contained none of the curls or softness she usually wore. She'd aged a decade since he'd last seen her.

She picked at her food, barely speaking a word.

Morgan attempted to engage her in various conversations, and Abby inquired after the christening gowns they had made for the twins, but she barely muttered a response. It seemed as though she was caught in a dreary, far-off place, unreachable by anyone.

At long last, the trio retired to the drawing room. Morgan shot a worried look at Abby before proposing a game of faro. He probably should have suggested charades instead, a pastime his mother had always liked, but he wanted to see how she'd react to a game Jasper had enjoyed. Was she ready to speak of her son, at least a little?

Her stricken gaze darted to his, and he caught a sheen of tears in her eyes before she quickly excused herself, muttering something about a headache.

Morgan mentally kicked himself. He hadn't meant to be cruel or unkind. Speaking of Jasper with Abby had brought a peace to Morgan's soul he'd never felt in the silent months after his father's death. He wanted to share that feeling with his mother, but how could he when she was determined to escape all thoughts of her son?

It pained him to see her so low.

"She makes me feel guilty for smiling and laughing," said Abby quietly. "Am I wrong to do so?"

Morgan considered the question before responding. "How would Jasper want you to feel?"

She nodded. They both knew the answer to that. "Perhaps if we keep trying, we can help her to smile again as well."

"Perhaps." Morgan refrained from pointing out that if she still intended to leave after the documents had been signed, they didn't have much time. His mother would need Abby's smiles and laughter as much as he did, if not more so.

He'd just have to try harder to convince her to stay.

Morgan mustered a cheerful tone. "I only suggested faro because it was a favorite of Jasper's. I don't really care for it. How about a stroll through the gardens instead?"

Abby pulled her black shawl tighter about her shoulders, as though the thought of venturing outside made her cold. "What about a game of Snapdragon? I've never played before, but I've always wanted to give it a go. It sounds exciting."

Morgan disagreed. He'd played it once and swore he'd never do so again. "Plucking raisins from a burning bowl of brandy is anything but exciting. We'll just burn our fingers and tongues. Besides, it's only September. Christmas is ages away."

"There is no law that says we can't play it now." She leaned forward and gave his hand a squeeze with her cold fingers. "Tell me you aren't the least bit tempted."

"I'm not the least bit tempted." Morgan looked down at their hands. This was the first time she'd voluntarily touched him, and he was glad to see—or rather, *feel*—it. She was no longer skittish around him, which was a good thing. Brothers and sisters *should* feel at ease in one another's company.

"You're freezing." He took her hand between both of his and began rubbing some warmth back into it.

Her smile seemed to freeze in place as she glanced from their clasped hands to his face. In that moment, something almost palpable crackled between them, like a wayward spark from a flame threatening to land somewhere it shouldn't, possibly even start a fire of its own.

Morgan swallowed. Perhaps he was beginning to feel a little too at ease with his sister-in-law.

He slowly relinquished her hand, then stood to stoke the fire. In an effort to dispel the awkward tension, he said, "How about a compromise? If you choose a different game for this evening, I will play Snapdragon with you on Christmas Eve." He didn't ask if she would be at Oakley on Christmas Eve or if she was still set on leaving. He merely waited.

"I'm beginning to think you are a spoilsport," she said at last, neither confirming nor quieting his concerns. But at least she'd made a valiant attempt to sound unaffected by his . . . caress.

Good gads, that's what he'd done, wasn't it? Caressed his brother's wife.

Widow, he quickly amended, as though that somehow made it better.

"I think the fire is well stoked, my lord," Abby said, her tone hinting at amusement.

Belatedly, Morgan realized he'd tossed in several logs. The fire practically roared, sending billows of heat into the room. At this rate, he'd have to open a window soon. He set aside the log he'd been about to throw in and brushed his hands together to remove the debris.

"That ought to warm you up," he said.

Her eyes danced with merriment as she watched him. "That was most thoughtful of you."

"We can't have you taking a chill, now can we?" The moment the words left his mouth, Morgan berated himself for behaving like a fool. One would think he'd never been around an attractive woman.

"Well," said Abby, her lips pressed together in thought. "Since Snapdragon is apparently too dangerous, what about Spillikins? Or are you concerned I'll stab myself with one of the sticks?"

"I'm a little concerned you'll stab me with one," he said.

She laughed, and Morgan realized just how much he loved that sound. It brightened his world and made him want to join in, or at least say something to make her giggle again.

As he moved to collect the game, he decided she should definitely not feel guilty about laughing. It would do his mother good to laugh as well.

Later, when they took turns extracting individual sticks from a mound, they exchanged more stories, teased, and talked. Morgan could have stayed in that room all night, but once he caught Abby covering her mouth with her palm in an effort to stifle a yawn, he became a spoilsport again and insisted she take herself off to bed.

Only after she'd gone did he realize he couldn't remember the last time he'd felt so much joy.

NINE

ABBY JERKED AWAKE to a loud clap of thunder. She blinked a moment or two to orient herself, then threw off her bed clothes and ran to the window, smiling when she saw lightning streak through the morning sky. As a child, thunderstorms had always frightened her, but she'd overcome those fears at some point and now enjoyed the fascinating display of lights and rumbles of thunder.

Beautiful.

A pair of blue-gray eyes the exact shade of the sky had a lot to do with her current mood, but so did Jasper. They may not have grown as close as she would have wished, but he'd taught her about the power of optimism, and she would always be grateful for the lesson.

It had been a little over a fortnight since her husband's body had been put to rest, yet how different she felt from those difficult days. Hope and peace filled her heart, and when another bolt of lightning lit the sky, a thrill as well.

Brigston hadn't mentioned the paperwork again, and Abby no longer felt anxious to sign anything. Her desire to leave dwindled more every day while her attachment to Brigston, Oakley, and even Jasper, odd as it sounded, increased. She'd enjoyed learning more about her late husband through the eyes of his brother and planned to pass the information along to her child someday. It was something she looked forward to, and how long had it been since she'd looked forward to anything?

Too long.

Abby rang for her maid and dressed quickly, anxious to get on with her day. Time with Brigston had become precious. Every day this past week, he'd planned something memorable. They'd played parlor games each evening, picnicked on a small rise overlooking the sea, and read passages from various books in the library. He'd taken her on a boat ride in the Solent, taught her to fish, and instructed her on estate enclosures and their benefits. Abby learned that he sincerely cared for his tenants and those he employed, took his responsibilities in parliament seriously, even though he despised London, and hated the feel of fish in his hands. Just thinking about the look of disgust on his face as he pried the hook from the mouth of the small mackerel made her giggle.

He was thoughtful, compassionate, amusing, and interesting, and she dreaded the day their time together would come to an end.

Thankfully, that day was not today.

Abby hummed quietly as she left her room behind. At the top of the stairs, she paused and peered down the long hallway towards Lady Brigston's bedchamber. Would her mother-in-law come out earlier than usual? She usually dined with them, but she never ate much and spoke hardly at all. The moment the servants removed their plates, she would make her excuses and return to her room. It was heartbreaking to see her looking so frail, worn, and miserable.

Abby realized she was gnawing on a fingernail, so she pulled if from her mouth and strode down the hall, stopping in front of the large, wooden door. She leaned an ear against it, listening for any sounds. There was nothing. No hushed voices, no quiet weeping, no clattering of a teacup. Only silence.

Was Lady Brigston still asleep, or was she listening to the storm rage outside, forlorn and alone?

Abby knocked quietly and practically jumped when she heard the woman's voice. "You may enter."

Nervously, Abby pushed open the door and walked inside, hoping her mother-in-law wouldn't take offense to the unexpected intrusion.

Lady Brigston sat in a gold-upholstered armchair by the fireplace, still in her dressing gown, though her hair had been combed, plaited, and twisted into a tight knot at the nape of her neck. It was a dreary sight. The heavy, rose-colored drapes were still drawn, and the only light in the room came from the fire crackling in the grate.

Lady Brigston glanced briefly at Abby before returning her gaze to the fire, not appearing the least bit surprised to see her daughter-in-law. She looked almost relieved. A rug covered her lap even though the room felt too warm. Abby wanted to douse the fire and open a window.

Instead, she sat down and clutched her fingers in her lap. She had no idea why she'd come. What words of comfort could she possibly have to ay?

"I despise thunderstorms," said Lady Brigston quietly.

The comment surprised Abby. Before she could rethink her reply, she blurted, "Jasper hated them as well," then grimaced and bit down hard on her tongue. She should have kept well enough alone.

Lady Brigston flinched a little, but to Abby's surprise, she asked, "Why do you say that?"

At least she didn't ask Abby to leave. That had to be a

positive sign. "Rain got in the way of his pursuits. He once told me that mud brought ruin upon everything from wheels and horses to boots and clothes. He called it, er . . . a dratted nuisance."

"That sounds like Jasper—all but *dratted*, that is," she added.

Abby smiled a little. "I may have tempered his language a little."

Lady Brigston emitted a noise that sounded like a rusty chuckle—a *pained*, rusty chuckle. "He had quite the tongue on him at times, didn't he?"

This was the most her mother-in-law had spoken in weeks, and the only time Abby had heard her mention Jasper. She could hardly believe it. "I wouldn't know. He rarely used strong language around me—only when it came to rain."

Lady Brigston's eyes clouded over, and her lips pressed into a thin, shaky line. "I miss him." The words were said so quietly, Abby could hardly hear them. "I've missed him since the day he left for school and made it clear he preferred the company of friends to his family's. I thought things would change when he brought you here. I thought . . ." Tears welled in her eyes, and she shook her head.

She looked so broken. It tore at Abby's heart, but what could she say to ease the pain? One wrong word and Abby could ruin the tentative friendship they'd developed.

"I want my son back," croaked Lady Brigston. "I want my husband back. I want life to feel happy and full again. And I want this horrid thunderstorm to subside."

Abby reached forward and placed her hand over Lady Brigston's, giving it a squeeze. "I used to hate thunderstorms as well, but not for the same reasons as Jasper. They frightened me."

"Not anymore?" Lady Brigston looked intrigued, and Abby shook her head.

"When I was eleven, a particularly bad storm brewed over Chillhorne House. I ran to the kitchen to cower with the servants until the worst of it had passed. My father was away at the time, and my guardian slumbered in her favorite chair, oblivious to my fears. The thunder was so loud. It rattled the windows, and I was sure lightning would strike the house any moment. But in the kitchen, surrounded by bustling servants, I felt safer. Mrs. Wood gave me a large serving of apple pie and asked me about my lessons. Not long after the storm passed, a maid rushed in, exclaiming for us to come and see. We followed her outside, and I saw the most glorious rainbow I have ever seen. The colors were vivid and radiant. I couldn't look away. In that moment, Mrs. Wood whispered something I'll never forget. She said, 'Rainbows only come after storms, you know.'"

Abby smiled at the memory. "After that, storms didn't scare me as much. They became the maker of rainbows." She paused before adding, "Your rainbow is on its way, my lady. I know it."

Lady Brigston smiled through her tears. "I hope you are right, my dear. Would you be so kind as to open my drapes?"

Happy to comply, Abby went to the window, praying a vibrant rainbow would be waiting on the other side of the curtains. But as soon as she pushed one aside, a lightning bolt split the sky, followed by an incredible clap of thunder.

Abby jumped before twisting back to her mother-in-law. "I'm sure it's a spectacular rainbow in the making."

Lady Brigston chuckled again, only this time it didn't sound quite as rusty or pained. "I shall hold you to that, my dear."

Not knowing what else to say, Abby looked around the

room. A large, still-life painting of roses hung above the mantle and gold paper covered the walls, but that was all. There were no brushes or combs on the dressing table, no miniatures of her late husband or family, and no books to be found anywhere. Only the small bouquet of wildflowers that Abby had picked the previous morning sat on her bedside table. She'd asked a maid to bring it up with her mother-in-law's breakfast tray and was glad to see that it was still here.

"Would you like for me to stay a while longer, my lady?" Abby asked.

"I'm sure you have better things to do than keep an old woman company."

"I'm sure I don't," said Abby, even as her stomach rumbled from hunger. Embarrassed, she placed her hand over top, and as she did so, felt something move within her.

She froze and waited for more. When another prod came, she grinned. "I think I just felt my child move. Oh, there it goes again. Would you like to feel?" Abby wanted to share this with someone, and Lady Brigston seemed the perfect choice. As soon as the lady's eyes widened, however, Abby knew she shouldn't have asked. Good grief, would she never learn?

In that moment, Abby missed Prudence dreadfully. Her friend would have been overjoyed to feel a babe squirm.

"Perhaps another time," said Lady Brigston. She must have noticed the disappointment in Abby's expression because she added, "It's an interesting sensation, is it not? Enjoy it while you can. In a few months the child's movements will become much more bothersome."

Abby wasn't sure how she could ever think of this feeling as bothersome, but she didn't argue. Her stomach rumbled again, sounding like distant thunder.

Lady Brigston waved Abby away with a flip of her wrist.

"Go and feed my grandchild, Abby. I am going to rest for now, but perhaps I'll join you for luncheon later."

Abby hesitated, not wanting to leave Lady Brigston alone while the storm continued to rage outside, but what other choice did she have? She'd been dismissed.

"I shall hope to see you at luncheon then," Abby said.

As she walked down the hall, she rested her hand over her stomach, hoping to feel her child move again. Before today, there had only been light fluttering, and she could never be sure if it was movement or not. Now, she knew with certainty. Her babe was alive and well and growing inside of her.

Brigston was already in the breakfast parlor, looking far too handsome as he studied some papers on the table in front of him. For a moment, Abby worried he finally had the document ready for her to sign, but as soon as he spotted her, he slid the papers aside and stood, greeting her with a smile. "I was wondering when you'd finally make it down, though how anyone could sleep through this storm is beyond me."

That smile. It wobbled her knees and stole her breath every time. Abby walked to the sideboard and began filling a plate, trying to think of something else. But it was no use. Thoughts of him came like the waves upon the sea.

She glanced down at her plate and frowned when she spotted a poached egg. *For pity's sake.* She despised poached eggs. Why had she taken that? Abby nearly returned it to the serving dish when she spied a footman watching her.

Stop behaving like a peagoose, she thought as she slathered apricot preserves on a scone, added a few slices of bacon to her plate, and tried to calm her racing pulse.

She took a seat across from Brigston and made the mistake of glancing at the small stack of papers on the table near his elbow.

He must've noticed because he said, "Just some mundane estate business." He cleared his throat and added in a careful tone, "My solicitor informed me this morning that he should have the final draft of the annuity agreement ready for you to sign tomorrow."

"He's finished already?" Abby tried to sound properly surprised, but her voice came out unnaturally high. What was the matter with her? Only a week prior, she would have signed her name and gathered her belongings with all possible speed. What had changed? Was it Brigston? His mother? Jasper? *Her*?

Everything, she realized. She didn't want to part with Brigston, his mother, or Jasper's memories. She wanted to belong here at Oakley. She wanted her child to belong. But how could she remain when she was on the brink of losing her heart to her brother-in-law?

"He would have been finished sooner, but I discovered a few errors in earlier drafts that needed to be altered."

Abby had no idea what sort of alterations he'd felt the need to make. Marriage contracts could take days or even weeks to negotiate, but what was there to negotiate now? She'd gratefully accept whatever sum Brigston saw fit to bestow upon her.

"How can I thank you for your generosity?" she asked.

"By agreeing to stay at Oakley, at least until your confinement comes to an end. I still owe you that game of Snapdragon, remember." He smiled to show he was teasing, but there was a hint of truth in his eyes. Or perhaps she only imagined it.

Abby turned her attention to her plate, surprised to see that only the poached egg remained. She set her fork down and swallowed. The time had come for her to make a decision. What should she choose? What would be best for everyone involved?

Abby thought of her mother-in-law and the conversation they'd had that morning. She remembered her smile, chuckle, and the hope that had flitted across her features, along with the look of shock at Abby's suggestion to feel her child move. It hadn't been the desired response, but it had been a response. Would she continue responding with only Brigston here?

Somehow, Abby doubted it. Perhaps her mother-in-law needed her. Perhaps Abby needed her mother-in-law.

"I was only teasing, Abby. You need not feel—"

"I'd like to stay," she blurted. "At least for a little longer. It feels wrong to leave Lady Brigston in such a state, especially if there is something I can do to ease her sorrow. I would like to try to help her, at least for another few weeks."

Brigston rested his elbows on the table. His hair fell across his forehead in that dashing way she was growing to love. She wanted to rest her cheek against his and smell that citrus and spice that had become so familiar to her. *Tell me you want me to stay forever, and I'll do it,* she thought.

"You've cheered me a great deal, and I believe you can help Mother as well, but I worry that you will make her more attached to you, and it will be harder on her in the end. As much as I hate to say it, if you only plan to remain with us another fortnight, perhaps it would be best if you left now."

Those were not the words Abby had expected or wanted him to say. They caused her pain and sorrow, mostly because she knew he was right. The attachment went both ways. As difficult as it would be to leave now, another fortnight would be dreadful.

But she wasn't ready to say goodbye either.

Brigston's warm hand captured hers, sending shivers of delight up her arms. When she lifted her gaze, his eyes were warm as well.

"Stay," he said quietly. "At least until March."

Abby felt herself nodding even before she had made up her mind. It was a strange sensation—her body responding one way while her mind cried out something else.

Six months. So much could go wrong in that amount of time.

So much could go right.

"March it is," said Abby quietly. It was the only choice she could make. She just prayed it wouldn't be a mistake.

Brigston's answering grin lightened her concerns and made her believe, even for a moment, that it had been the right choice—at the very least, the happier one.

He relinquished her hand and relaxed against the back of his seat, draping one arm over the chair adjacent to him. His casual demeanor was disappointing in a way. Did he not fear becoming too attached to her as well?

Apparently not.

"I propose a game of shuttlecock," he said suddenly, pulling her from her thoughts.

Abby blinked, sure she'd heard wrong. Shuttlecock? Today? Was he in earnest? Although the thunder had subsided, the rain had not. The window pane behind him still bled with constant droplets of water.

"Are you suggesting we play in the rain?" she asked, ready to feel his forehead for a fever.

His answering smile was both devilish and mischievous. "I'm suggesting we play in the ballroom."

Abby waited for him to laugh or say he was only jesting, but he didn't. "Are you mad? Your mother would never countenance such a thing."

"What she does not know she cannot scold us for later," he said, tossing her own words back at her.

Abby laughed. She loved that he remembered things

she'd once said, teased her about them, and sometimes used them against her. In truth, the thought of playing shuttlecock in the ballroom *did* excite her, but . . . but what? This was Brigston's home, for pity's sake. If he thought batting around rackets in the ballroom was an appropriate way to spend the remainder of the morning, who was she to argue?

"Do you remember when you inquired about Jasper's least favorite childhood game the other day?" he said.

"You mean the game you wouldn't disclose to me?" Abby was still annoyed at him for that. What was the harm in revealing Jasper's most disliked game? He'd been forthcoming about his brother's *favorite* game—Blind Man's Bluff—but the moment she asked for the opposite, Brigston had become most mysterious, refusing to give her a straight answer.

"I gave you some clues," he said.

If by *clues* he meant that he'd turned a simple question into a blasted riddle, she'd have to agree.

Clue #1: *Jasper's least favorite childhood game was my favorite.*

Clue #2: *It's a game that requires great dexterity and . . . juggling.*

How could Abby possibly guess from such vague hints? Great dexterity? Juggling? He wouldn't even tell her if he meant figurative juggling or literal. Her mind conjured up the most absurd games—everything from balancing a pile of books on one's head to keeping a frog from leaping off the end of a stick. This was the very reason she despised riddles. They plagued her mind until the answer revealed itself, which rarely happened unless someone gave her more obvious clues.

It had taken her hours to rid her mind of the dratted conundrum, so why was he bringing it up again?

"Your ridiculous clues didn't help at all," she said with a frown.

He laughed, clearly enjoying her frustration. "Consider my suggestion for today's amusement as another clue."

Abby rolled her eyes, wondering why she hadn't guessed it sooner. What a nincompoop she could be. "Shuttlecock was Jasper's least favorite game?"

"And my favorite." His eyes danced with humor. "Care to know why?"

"Not especially."

He answered anyway. "It's because I could always beat Jasper soundly. He used to despise me for it."

Judging by the gleam in his eyes, Brigston was excited about the prospect of trouncing her as well. It pricked at her pride and sense of competition. Did he think he'd beat her so easily?

"What an interesting coincidence," she said. "Shuttlecock happens to be my favorite childhood game for that same reason." In truth, she'd played it only once with Prudence when they couldn't think of anything else amusing to do, but Abby hadn't been completely terrible at it—or perhaps Prudence had just been more terrible.

Brigston's lips twitched, probably because he saw through her bluff and didn't believe a word. "What a fortuitous coincidence. All these years I've searched for a worthy opponent only to discover she's been under my nose these past few months."

"Fortuitous indeed," Abby said, thinking the game didn't sound nearly as exciting as it had before. "My only concern is whether or not the doctor would approve of me participating in such a . . . er, vigorous activity."

"I considered that as well, but then I remembered my Mother introduced me to the game only a few months before her lying in with Jasper. If her doctor gave her leave to play at that juncture, surely he wouldn't see a problem with you doing so now, especially if I promise not to make it easy on you."

He was baiting her and she, like a fool, was letting him. Abby nearly blurted that she didn't need him or anyone else to make the game easier for her, but that would have been a third lie, and two lies per conversation were her limit. Goodness, he was aggravating.

"Very well," she finally relented. "Shuttlecock in the ballroom it is."

"You sound perturbed. Never say you're worried you'll lose."

"I'm more concerned I'll fling this poached egg at you if you continue teasing me," said Abby, thinking it wasn't a bad idea. Better that than trying to gag it down her unwilling throat.

He laughed and rose, pushing his chair in. "I know a dismissal when I hear one. You'll find me in the ballroom once you've finished with breakfast. Do try and cheer yourself up before then."

"Only if you try to humble yourself," Abby muttered as he turned to leave.

She didn't mean for him to hear, but he grinned back at her. "Won't you be the one to do that with your exceptional shuttlecock skills?"

Abby picked up the egg, ready to fling it in his direction, but he laughed and quit the room before she could gather the courage. It was probably for the best. They'd already given the servants plenty to gossip about.

TEN

MORGAN STOOD IN the ballroom, leaning against the wall near one of the large windows that looked out onto the balcony. He tossed the shuttlecock high into the air and caught it with the same hand while waiting for Abby to join him. What could possibly be taking her so long? Had she decided to change gowns? Was she punishing him for teasing her earlier? Or had she decided not to play after all?

Morgan should be shut away in his study with his bailiff, but he had no desire to do so this morning—or any morning really. Lately, it had been too easy to find excuses and ignore his responsibilities, which was odd. Only weeks earlier, he'd been in such a rush to get everything done.

"You really intend to play?" asked a lovely voice.

Morgan grinned at the sound, something that happened a great deal in Abby's company. He looked up to find her standing across the ballroom, looking beautiful but much too pale. Black did not suit her at all, and he couldn't wait for the day she could do away with the drab color.

"I will if you will."

Her eyes darted from the shuttlecock in his hand to the rackets at his feet. "Since I am at a disadvantage, being in a delicate condition and all, I think it only fair that you have an impairment as well."

He pushed away from the wall and walked towards her. "Do you intend to whack me over the head with a racket and make me dizzy?"

"I was thinking more along the lines of a blindfold," she suggested. "It might be less painful for you."

"Unless I trip or run into a wall."

"True."

He stopped a few feet away. "Your skills must be pitiful indeed if it'll take blinding me to make the match fair."

Her lips puckered into a frown, and he felt the greatest urge to kiss it away. *Careful, old goat,* he thought, knowing he was treading on dangerous ground and had been for a while now. He should be putting distance between them, not thinking up new excuses to spend time with her.

Which begged the question: Why the devil had he convinced her to stay at Oakley until March?

For your mother's sake. And Abby's.

It was true enough. Abby needed a family as much as his mother needed a daughter and a grandchild.

"If you're truly opposed to being blindfolded—"

"I am."

"Then . . . well, I suppose you can complete some sort of dance movement each time it is your turn, before you strike the shuttlecock."

He stared at her a moment, expecting her to laugh or say she was only jesting. Surely her suggestion sounded as absurd to her as it did to him. "A dance movement," he repeated.

"We are in a ballroom."

"I think I'd prefer the whacking."

She laughed. "Come now, my lord. I'm certain you are a

good dancer. How difficult is a bow, plié, or demi-jeté? It really does not matter what you do, only that you don't repeat any of the steps."

His eyes widened. "If that is the stipulation, this game will be over after a dozen strikes. I'm not well versed in dance movements, Lady Jasper."

She waved her hand as though it didn't matter. "I give you leave to invent as many steps as you need. Now, do you wish to play or not?"

Morgan rubbed the back of his neck. He had never cared much for dancing, nor did he have any desire to invent new steps. But should he refuse, he could only imagine what Abby would think of next. Would he be asked to play on his knees or stand on his head? Would she require him to drink a glass of port after every point? Would they argue about it the remainder of the day and never get around to actually playing?

He supposed doing a few dance steps between hits would be harmless enough.

"Very well. If it pleases you, I shall make a fool of myself before every turn, but only if you hit the shuttlecock high enough to make it possible."

"Agreed."

Morgan tossed her the shuttlecock then removed his coat and slung it over the back of a chair in the corner. Then he retrieved the rackets and passed one to her before bowing gallantly.

"Ladies first," he said, gesturing for her to begin.

She appeared a little awkward as she tossed up the shuttlecock and hit it with the racket, but it flew towards the ceiling, giving Morgan enough time to drop into a plié before returning it.

She burst out laughing, covering her mouth with her free hand while the shuttlecock fell to the floor at her feet.

Morgan ignored the jeering. "One point for me," he said.

That put a stop to her laughter. "But I was distracted."

"If you find my dancing too distracting, perhaps I should desist."

"No, no," she said quickly. "I will be better prepared from this point forward. Let's give it another go." She picked up the shuttlecock and sent it flying once more.

This time, Morgan waltzed before returning it. She giggled only a little before hitting it again, and play continued with Morgan bowing, triple-stepping, and gliding across the ballroom floor. Each dance movement became more exaggerated than the last, and her giggles more prominent. When he began making up steps of his own, she laughed so hard she missed the shuttlecock more often than not. Before long, the score was eighteen to two in Morgan's favor. She didn't seem to care that she was losing, and Morgan enjoyed making her laugh.

For his next move, he dropped to one knee, then launched himself across the floor to get to the shuttlecock in time. It soared high, bounced off the ceiling, and landed squarely on a candle in the chandelier.

"Of all the rotten luck," Morgan muttered as he pulled himself to his feet and studied the fixture, which towered at least four or five meters above. They'd need a ladder to retrieve it.

Abby moved to stand next to him, looking first at the fixture and then at him. "If memory serves, it's minus twenty points for losing a shuttlecock to a chandelier." She clicked her tongue and shook her head in a sorrowful way. "I suppose that means I win."

Even in her black gown, she looked fetching—flushed cheeks, hair loosened from the exercise, and bright blue eyes.

At some point during their play, the storm must have abated. Light cascaded through the windows behind her, making her look angelic, even in black.

You're stunning, he thought.

She broke eye contact first, pressing her lips together and looking uncomfortable. He realized then that he'd been staring. Morgan drew in a breath to clear his head, trying to remember what she'd said. Oh, yes. Minus twenty points.

He bent to retrieve his racket. "Your memory is faulty," he said. "First you remember being good at shuttlecock when you're actually dreadful at it, and now there's the matter of that nonexistent rule. Twenty points indeed."

"If you are allowed to invent dance movements, I should be allowed to create a rule."

"The dancing was your idea, not mine."

She folded her arms. "Jasper would agree with me."

Morgan had no doubt that he would, just as he had no doubt Abby would not budge, no matter how absurd her arguments were. He glanced up at the chandelier again. "How about a compromise? If I can knock the shuttlecock down, you must acknowledge me as champion. If not, I'll concede my defeat."

She appeared skeptical. "How do you intend to knock it down?"

"With my uncanny dexterity," he answered, taking careful aim. He tossed his racket toward the shuttlecock, but instead of dislodging it, it knocked a candle from its perch and became wedged in the chandelier.

He muttered a curse and Abby laughed. "Would you like to toss up my racket as well, my lord? Perhaps you've just invented a new style of chandeliers. We can call them shuttleliers. What do you think? We can say it's a fixture that provides light as well as a diverting game, assuming one can extract the accessories."

Morgan stared at her for a moment before he burst out laughing. He wasn't sure what he found so amusing—something in her tone or facial expression? Perhaps it was the ridiculousness of the entire conversation. Whatever the reason, mirth poured out of him like a well that had ruptured. He bent forward and clutched his stomach, feeling tears seep from the corners of his eyes.

Gads, it felt good to laugh.

When he finally straightened, he looked at Abby. She was a wonder. When he considered his initial opinion of her—that she was nothing more than an empty-headed fool—he felt ashamed. *He'd* been the fool. Abby was intelligent, witty, and good—the kind of good that made her vibrant and exquisite. What would he do if she ever decided to leave?

What will you do if she doesn't?

The thought prodded his feet in her direction. He wanted to touch her, circle her waist with his hands, and pull her close. He wanted to smell the scent of apples that lingered in the air around her. He wanted to taste her lips.

He reached out to touch her face. "Abby, I—"

A throat cleared loudly, and Morgan's hand fell to his side. His mother stood near the entrance to the ballroom, her features stern and disapproving.

"A word, if you please, Morgan."

The realization of what he'd nearly done washed over Morgan like a cold rain shower. He'd been so sure he could keep Abby at arm's length, so sure he could keep his growing feelings for her in check. He should have known better.

Morgan nearly growled in frustration. He'd finally found a woman he wanted to pursue, only he was not at liberty to do so. If his mother hadn't arrived when she had . . .

He bowed briefly to Abby before following his mother from the room. She didn't speak until they were in the library with the door closed. She stood in front of the far window with her back to him for a few moments before turning around to face him.

"Do you have feelings for her?"

Caught off guard, Morgan stiffened. He hadn't expected her to be so direct, but surely she'd already seen the answer to that. Any man would have to be blind and deaf not to develop feelings for Abby.

"We have become friends, Mother," he said in clipped tones. "Nothing more."

"Are you certain about that?"

"Yes."

She shot him a look that implied she wasn't convinced. "She is your *sister*, Morgan."

"She's my sister-*in-law*." Why he'd felt the need to clarify that, he didn't know, but the words slipped out before he could swallow them.

"Not in the eyes of the law."

Morgan sighed and dropped to a chair, running his fingers through his hair. "I know, Mother." Before, Lord Hardwicke's Marriage Act had been nothing more to him than an inconsequential law. Now, he thought it an absurd creation of foolish minds.

"I have no intention of dallying with her, Mother," he said, ready to be finished with this conversation.

"What *are* your intentions? I saw the way you were looking at her just now, and it was neither friendly nor brotherly. Since you cannot marry her, what am I to think?"

Morgan wanted to turn his back on his mother and walk from the room, mostly because he didn't have an answer for her. What *were* his intentions? "I hold Abby in the highest of regard and would never dishonor her. We were merely playing a game of shuttlecock, that is all."

"Shuttlecock," she scoffed. "I saw no rackets or shuttlecock."

Morgan opened his mouth to explain, then promptly closed it. Apparently, she hadn't seen the racket in Abby's hand or noticed the additions to their chandelier. Perhaps someday he would enlighten her, but that day would not be today.

"Abby doesn't feel like she belongs at Oakley. Only last week, she expressed her desire to leave. I didn't think you'd want that, so I made an effort to seek her out, hoping to help her feel more at home." It was true enough. He'd started off with that intent, at least. Somewhere along the line his feelings had become muddied, but he wasn't about to admit as much to his mother.

Some of the color drained from her face, and all sternness left her voice. "Leave? Before the child is born? What will she do? Where will she go?"

Morgan's heart softened at her obvious distress. Despite her reservations with her daughter-in-law, Abby must have grown on her at least a little. Or was it the child his mother did not wish to part with?

"If it eases your concerns, I've managed to convince her to stay through the remainder of her confinement and lying in. Beyond that, I wouldn't be surprised if she returns to the care of Lord and Lady Knave."

That seemed to appease her, at least a little, but it didn't appease Morgan. How could it when either way, he lost? Stay or go, Abby could never be his. Jasper had seen to that the moment he'd married her.

His mother's jaw firmed, and her eyes shone with determination. "I have closeted myself away long enough. As of this moment, I will do so no longer."

"Glad to hear it." Morgan didn't know what she meant to do from this point forward, but he was pleased to see some of her pluck return. Perhaps she would look after Abby from here on out, and he could use the time to determine if his life would be any easier without her at its center.

He stood to leave, pausing with his hand on the library door. "Will you make sure Abby doesn't convince one of the grooms to let her ride? She seems to think the doctor is wrong to keep her from that particular exercise." The memory of her flashing blue eyes and insistence that she knew better than any doctor would be forever branded in his mind. He'd miss their daily interactions. He'd miss her.

"Of course she cannot ride. She probably shouldn't have played shuttlecock, if indeed she did," said his mother pointedly.

Morgan looked back at her. "I recall the day you played with me, not long before Jasper was born."

She frowned for a moment before her brow cleared. A hint of a smile softened her features. "I suppose I did, didn't I? How I despised the restrictions that came with confinement, especially the fact that your father could do whatever he wished when I could not."

If only Morgan could do whatever *he* wished. "I must see to estate business now. I'll leave Abby in your capable hands." It wasn't what Morgan wanted to do, but it's what he *should* want. Something needed to change. He'd nearly tossed caution to the wind and kissed her earlier. What had he been thinking?

It was past time to refocus his mind on something other than his sister-in-law.

ELEVEN

ABBY HAD NEVER felt more stifled. After the shuttlecock fiasco, Lady Brigston became her shadow. Not only did she plan every second of every hour of every day, but she was in the breakfast parlor when Abby first came down, and she didn't leave the drawing room in the evenings until Abby or Brigston retired.

She was a taskmaster, of sorts, keeping Abby busy with various *ladylike* activities. They embroidered cushions, sketched, painted, gardened, and walked about the grounds. At first, Abby was pleased to see Lady Brigston in better spirits, but as the days passed and Abby's interactions with Brigston dwindled to almost nothing, she decided she didn't care much for the change.

She missed Brigston. Their brief exchanges in the breakfast parlor or dining room did not suffice. With his mother's constant supervision, conversation was stilted at best. Abby ached for the easy camaraderie they'd once shared. She wanted to walk with him, play shuttlecock with him, read with him, and laugh with him. Lady Brigston was enjoyable enough to be around, but she wasn't her son. Abby didn't smile as much, and her heart never danced.

One particular morning, Abby sat near the drawing

room window, her attention caught by Brigston, who was returning to the stables on the back of his horse. He rode with grace and looked dashing dressed in all black. If only she could have joined him on the ride that morning.

Lady Brigston bustled into the room, her black taffeta skirts swishing in a grating manner. Abby did her best to hide her frustration, but could she not enjoy the solace for at least a few minutes? She was tempted to complain of a headache and spend the day in her room, just to be free of the woman's constant hovering. But Abby would never really do such a thing. Her mother-in-law was simply craving the distraction company brought. Abby had once felt the same.

"Only see what just arrived, Abby," said Lady Brigston, clearly excited about something. She cradled a pile of lace, fabrics, and ribbons in her arms and held them up for Abby's inspection. "I ordered these from London months ago, and they've finally come."

Curiosity piqued, Abby perused the various folds of fabric, oohing and ahhing at the white embroidered muslin and pastel-colored cottons—there was a blue and white polka-dot, cream with little peach flowers, and a green fabric covered with small, black diamonds.

"What do you plan to do with these, my lady?" Abby asked.

Lady Brigston pointed to the pastels. "I thought we could make some small quilts from these. And this"—she lifted the white muslin and smiled—"is for the christening gown. Isn't it lovely?"

Abby's fingers stilled on the muslin. *For the christening gown.*

The words echoed in her mind while her stomach twisted into knots. Abby stared at the closest relation she had to a mother, praying she'd purchased the fabric for someone else.

"A christening gown for whom?" she asked quietly.

Lady Brigston chuckled. "Silly girl. My grandchild, of course."

But it's not really your grandchild, Abby thought as the cold reality washed over her. She shouldn't have asked for clarification. She should have just imagined it was for a tenant's child or member of the local parish so she could continue pushing the truth to the far recesses of her mind.

No, it was time. It was past time. Her mother-in-law needed to know the truth before she took a pair of shears to that beautiful fabric.

"Is something the matter, child?" Lady Brigston asked. "You seem rather pale."

Nausea overtook Abby, and she clutched her stomach. "Forgive me, my lady, but I am feeling suddenly unwell. Pray excuse me."

Abby dashed from the room and raced up the stairs. Once there, she hurried past the door of her bedchamber, trotted down the servants' staircase, and escaped out the back door. A blast of chilly air met her, but she paid it no mind as she strode towards the stables.

MORGAN HAD JUST finished speaking with a groom about his horse when Abby burst into the stall, looking flushed and beautiful and . . . black. How tired he was growing of that color.

He forced his attention back to his animal. "If you have come to ask Duncan to saddle a horse for you, remember that I forbid it."

When she didn't laugh or return his playful banter, Brigston realized something was wrong. He looked at her more closely, noticing her troubled expression and worry-filled eyes.

"You must tell your mother the truth this instant," she blurted, wringing her hands.

It took a moment for Morgan to realize what she meant. The groom lingered not far away, his ear turned in their direction. Gads, this was not the time or the place for a conversation of this nature, but Abby was obviously too distraught to realize that.

What the deuce had happened?

He tossed the brush aside and took her by the arm, saying loud enough for the groom to hear, "Would you care to accompany me on a walk about the grounds, Abby?"

She followed his gaze to the groom and winced, then pressed her lips together and nodded, allowing him to lead her from the stables. He took her through the woods until they reached a clearing that was out of sight from the house and stables.

"Please, Brigston, you must tell her."

He couldn't understand her sudden need for haste. It had been weeks since they discussed this, and the birth was still months away. In truth, Morgan's thoughts had been more occupied with Abby than her child. That had been the last thing on his mind.

"Has something occurred?" he asked.

"Yes," she cried. "Your mother ordered fabric for the christening gown. From London! It arrived this morning, and she wants to start on it directly. You promised you would tell her before she began making that gown, and now she's probably working on it as we speak!"

"Abby, calm yourself." Morgan rested his hands on her shoulders, but she shook them off and began pacing.

"I feel wretched keeping this from her, and that fabric! I

can only imagine the price she must have paid. She is so excited to welcome her first grandchild, and she has no idea it isn't really hers."

Her voice broke, and Morgan could see that tears would soon follow. He caught her arm and turned her around to face him. When she didn't pull away again, he gently pulled her against him. His hand trailed up and down her back in an effort to comfort her, but as she melted against him and wrapped her arms around his waist, all he could think was how good it felt to finally hold her. He tucked her in closer, not caring about the consequences.

"She's in better spirits now," Abby continued, her voice muffled against his shirt. "It will only be worse the longer we wait."

"I know, Abby," he said softly. "I know."

She peered up at him, looking anxious and lovely and altogether too trusting. "You'll tell her then?"

Unable to deny her anything, he nodded and was rewarded with a look of relief, followed by a tenuous smile. Without thinking, his fingers brushed across her cheek in a caress. How soft she felt.

"I've missed you," she said in that honest way he loved.

"I've missed you, too."

Abby closed her eyes and leaned her face into his hand. "I like it when you touch me. After what happened to me, I didn't think I'd ever want anyone to touch me again, but it's different with you."

The beat of Morgan's heart pulsed in his ears. She smelled like apples and felt like heaven. What was keeping them apart? She was his *sister-in-law*, not his sister. They were not blood relatives by any stretch of the imagination. He didn't even know of her existence before last season.

What idiot decided that marriage between sisters-in-law

and brothers-in-law should be prohibited? No one with any amount of sense.

Morgan suddenly didn't care any longer. His fingers moved beneath her chin, and he gently lifted it. When she didn't pull away, he slowly lowered his mouth to hers. He kissed her tentatively at first, but when she sighed and moved her soft lips across his, what control he still possessed fled. He tightened his arms around her as his mouth explored hers. Every touch evoked a new sensation. He was flying and falling at the same time.

This was right. It felt right. It had to be right.

You're wrong, said a nagging voice in his head.

He kissed Abby harder, trying to silence the voice, telling himself it was the law that was in error, not him. How could this possibly be wrong? She fit so perfectly in his arms, as though she had been made especially for him.

If you care about her, you will stop now.

This time, Morgan couldn't ignore the voice or the consequences he'd bring upon those closest to him should he continue down this path.

With a muttered curse, he broke free, despising himself for doing something that would undoubtedly bring Abby additional pain. He was a selfish, unforgivable cad.

"I'm sorry, Abby. I should not have done that."

"Why?" Some of her hair had fallen to her shoulders, and she appeared befuddled and shaken.

"It was wrong."

"It didn't feel wrong."

He nearly smiled, having thought the same thing himself, but . . . "How can it be right when the law prohibits us from marrying?"

"It doesn't truly prohibit us, does it?" she asked. "I know of a man and woman in a similar situation who were married in a church in London."

"Yes, but did they tell the parson they were brother and sister-in-law? If they had, he would have never permitted the union."

He released her and massaged the back of his neck. This wasn't just about him. It was about her, his mother, his future family, even Jasper. It felt like a betrayal of everything he knew to be right, and no matter which way he looked at it, Morgan couldn't see how it could possibly end well for either of them. Only problems and complications arose. Regrets.

"Your reputation would be in tatters," he tried.

"I don't care a fig about my reputation."

He nearly said, *Then why did you elope with my brother?* but bit his tongue before the words came out. Even if she didn't want to admit it, she *did* care. They both did.

"Was this man you speak of a marquess of means?" he asked. "Was the woman a well-bred lady?"

Her eyes sparked with stubborn indignation. "Why should that matter?"

"It's not just our reputations that would be affected, Abby," he said. "You're correct in thinking we could post the banns in a parish where we are not known and legally marry in spite of the law. We may even be able to keep it to ourselves for a time. But eventually, the ton will learn of it, along with my greedy cousin, and suppose he decides to contest the marriage. What then? All it would take is for one person to make it an issue, and our union would be voided. Our children would become illegitimate in an instant, and Markus would become heir. Is that a risk you're willing to take?"

The fight and determination seemed to seep out of her in an instant, leaving behind a pained, sorrowful expression. "No," she said quietly.

Morgan groaned inwardly, not wanting to leave things

like this. There was some hope to be had, after all, even if it was only a granule. Still, he hesitated bringing it up.

"Abby, if the child you're carrying is male, he will legally take the place of my cousin as next in line. If that is the case, perhaps no one will go to the trouble of contesting our marriage. But it would be a gamble, and if your child is female . . ." his voice drifted off.

"I would never put you in that position, Brigston, nor did I realize the full extent of the consequences. Pray forgive me. I merely got caught up in the moment."

"Abby . . ." Morgan couldn't stand the thought of letting her walk away. He wanted to take her in his arms once more and never let go. But he couldn't. As much as it wounded both of them, this was the only choice they could make. "If there was any other way . . ."

"I understand." She folded her arms against her chest and shivered. "It's gotten chilly all of a sudden, hasn't it?"

Morgan began to remove his jacket for her to wear, but she stopped him with a shake of her head. "That will only cause more talk."

"Let me walk you back to the house."

She shook her head again. "It would be better if I returned alone." She dropped into a quick curtsy, and without looking at him again, said, "Good day, my lord."

Every instinct in Morgan told him to run after her and not give up, to find a solution that left no room for future regrets. But there was none to be had, and as much as he didn't want to care about the law or his duty or anything else, he did care. He had to care. It was his responsibility to care.

He muttered another oath under his breath, kicked a fallen log, then strode in the opposite direction of the house. He needed a good, long walk to cool his temper and clear his head.

ABBY DIDN'T RETURN to the house directly. She circled around back and walked aimlessly through the woods until tears stopped streaming down her cheeks.

Why had Brigston kissed her? Before that moment, she'd had no real expectations, only dreams of endless days at his side or fantasies of being wrapped in his arms. But that's all they'd been—wishful thinking. As soon as he'd pulled her close, however, wonderful possibilities ignited in her mind. *That kiss.* It had been like nothing she'd ever experienced. She'd wanted it to go on and on, without end. She'd felt wounds heal and anxieties fade. And the sense of belonging—it was how she'd always imagined coming home should feel.

When had Brigston become home to her?

Abby should have known better than to hope. Every time she allowed herself to do so, disappointment inevitably followed. Life seemed to contain more bad than good, more sorrow than joy. It was how it had always been for her, how it probably always would be. Would this cycle never cease?

A tiny foot nudged the inside of her belly, reminding her that she still had something good in her life. Abby needed that reminder. She placed her hand protectively over the top and whispered, "As long as I live, you will never feel alone. I promise you that."

Only then did it occur to her that she wasn't alone anymore either.

The thought lifted her chin and stiffened her shoulders. She'd suffered through far worse than this, and life hadn't beaten her yet. For the sake of her child, she would keep up the fight. It was the only thing to do.

TWELVE

ABBY CRIED OFF from dinner, not because she wanted to avoid Brigston, although she'd rather not face him anytime soon, but because she had the most abominable headache. A slight turn of her neck sent waves of pain through her head. Moving hurt, speaking hurt, even sunlight hurt. She'd begged Evie to draw the curtains. Lying perfectly still with her eyes closed was the only way she tolerated the pain.

What had she done to deserve this?

Her maid brought cool cloths for her forehead and a tea that Monsuier Roch promised would cure even the worst headache. Abby forced herself to take a few sips, but oh the pain! Lady Brigston came in at some point—probably after dinner—with some soup, but Abby couldn't eat it. The thought of food churned her stomach.

"I can't," Abby squeaked, grimacing when fresh waves of pain thudded through her head.

"I understand," said her mother-in-law in a quiet voice. Abby heard some rummaging and then Lady Brigston's voice came again, still quiet. She sounded like she was reading something. A book. A story. Abby couldn't focus on the words, but amazingly enough, her mother-in-law's calm voice eventually soothed her into a fitful sleep that lasted only until she heard the door close. After that, she managed to sip some more tea and continued to suffer until late into the night when either the tea or sheer exhaustion crept in, and she finally slept. By morning, her headache had dwindled into a mere annoyance.

Thank heavens, she thought, hoping to never suffer in that way again.

On her bedside table, the soup had been replaced with a fresh cup of tea and some dry toast. Both were cold but still tasted good. Abby glanced at the clock, startled to see that it was nearly noon already. What had Monsieur Roch put in that tea? She looked at the cup at her side and decided not to drink anymore, choosing to take another bite of toast instead. Then she rang for her maid.

It was never difficult to decide what to wear since she only had a handful of black dresses to her name—most of which had come from Lady Brigston's trunks in the attic. She had planned to order a few more that would accommodate her growing figure, but she hadn't gotten around to doing it yet. Too many other things had occupied her mind.

She glanced in the looking glass with a frown, quickly pinching her cheeks to add some color to her complexion. How pale and sickly she always appeared in this color.

She sighed and turned away from her reflection. Brigston had surely told his mother the truth about the child by now, and Abby would be a coward if she did not go down and speak to her also. Lady Brigston deserved an explanation from her as well.

Her stomach in knots, she descended the staircase to the drawing room, wondering how her mother-in-law had reacted to the news. Had she been as understanding as Brigston had been, or had it upset her? Would she even speak to Abby this morning? Had the warmth in her expression turned cold?

Perhaps Abby should speak to Brigston first.

Coward, said a voice inside her head, prodding her feet into the room.

Lady Brigston sat on a cozy settee, humming quietly while she sewed neat stitches into the same white muslin she'd shown Abby yesterday.

She looked up and smiled. "I was only just thinking that I ought to look in on you. Are you feeling more the thing?"

Abby barely registered the question. She was still focused on the christening gown and its meaning. Had Lady Brigston come to terms with the news already? Did she still think of the child as Jasper's? Had all of Abby's fears been for naught? What had Brigston said to her?

"You appear to have more color," noted Lady Brigston.

"Er . . . yes. My headache has nearly subsided, I'm sure in part to Monsieur Roch's tea and to you. It was good of you to read to me last night. Thank you."

Lady Brigston waved a dismissive hand. "I used to get the most dreadful headaches. When they were at their worst, my late husband would read to me. I always found it soothing."

"As did I, my lady."

Lady Brigston smiled. "I am glad. Has your nausea subsided as well? You ran out of here like the devil was after you yesterday. Perhaps I should have followed, but I never liked an audience when I experienced bouts of sickness."

"I . . . yes, my lady. I am feeling much better now. Forgive me for leaving so abruptly."

"I understand completely, my dear," said Lady Brigston. "During my confinements, I would feel fine one moment and ill the next. It was quite vexing, to be sure, but it did not last forever. It's only a matter of time before it will subside completely for you. Do sit down. Are you hungry at all? Shall I ring for tea?"

"I've had some already," said Abby somewhat distractedly. Lady Brigston returned to her needlepoint while Abby watched her in confusion. How strange this was. She had been expecting a cold reception and an uncomfortable confrontation, but Lady Brigston was behaving as though nothing had changed, as though she had no idea about—

No.

Surely she knew. Brigston had made Abby a promise, and he was a man of his word—or, at least he'd always seemed to be.

She eyed her mother-in-law worriedly. "Have you spoken to Brigston lately, my lady?"

The woman continued to sew. "I haven't seen him this morning. Smithson mentioned he left in a hurry before sunrise."

"Did you not speak to him at dinner yesterday?"

Lady Brigston looked up from her needlepoint, her expression wary. "*Should* I have spoken to him?"

Abby tried to swallow the lump in her throat, but it didn't budge. Brigston hadn't told his mother anything. He hadn't kept his promise.

That hurt almost as much as his rejection had.

Lady Brigston set aside the christening gown and clasped her hands together, watching Abby with a firm, unwavering look. "You have never been one to mince words, Abby. Is there something you wish to tell me?"

"Yes," said Abby weakly, ready to rid herself of the weight she'd been carrying.

I will be the one to tell her when the time is appropriate, Brigston had said. *Please, Abby, you must trust me on this.*

She *had* trusted him. She'd agreed to keep quiet if he promised to explain everything to his mother *before* she began working on the christening gown. That was the bargain they'd made, the one he'd failed to follow through on.

Abby walked over to the doors and pulled them closed. Then she inhaled deeply, squared her shoulders, and turned around to meet her mother-in-law's gaze. She should never have listened to Morgan or Jasper. She should have told Lady Brigston the truth as soon as she'd crossed the threshold into this house.

"Yes," she said again, her voice stronger this time. "There is something I need to tell you before you put another stitch in that gown."

THIRTEEN

MORGAN RETURNED FROM an exhausting morning spent overseeing some repairs on a ditch. It had overrun during a storm the previous night and had flooded a tenant's fields. He could only pray the damage had not been too extensive or he'd need to recompense the man with funds he didn't have at the moment. Jasper's debts had been steeper than Morgan had initially realized.

He couldn't remember the last time he'd felt so physically and mentally drained. Perhaps if he'd slept better, but the crashes of thunder and thoughts of Abby had kept him awake much of the night. He was stripping off his gloves in the great hall when the door to the drawing room opened and Abby rushed out, looking pale and stricken. She glanced at him briefly before lifting her skirts and darting up the stairs.

He stared at her in confusion, wondering what had put her in such a state.

"Abby," he called out.

She stopped and stiffened, but only turned her head slightly to the side. "You promised you would tell her," she said before continuing up the stairs and out of sight.

Morgan muttered a curse under his breath as he tossed

his gloves and hat to a nearby footman. He strode into the drawing room, finding his mother standing with her back to him, her hands fisted at her sides.

Not a good sign.

"What did you say to her?" he demanded, almost afraid to hear her answer.

She spun around and glared at him, her eyes flashing. "Did you know?"

He sighed and blinked against the dryness in his eyes. "She informed me not long after Jasper's passing."

His mother gaped at him, the shock in her expression confirming what he'd already suspected. Either Abby had kept his involvement to herself or his mother hadn't given her the opportunity to explain much of anything. It was probably a combination of both. Morgan remembered his own reaction to Abby's confession well enough, along with the conclusions he'd initially drawn about her character. Thankfully, he'd listened to her entire tale before reacting too harshly. Judging by the way Abby had looked just now, his mother hadn't done the same.

"All this time you've let me carry on about my grand-child and a possible family resemblance when you knew it wasn't really Jasper's. Why would you keep this from me— your own mother?" Her voice was quiet and harsh, filled with pain. He'd expected this reaction. It was the reason he'd asked Abby not to tell her immediately. He just hadn't ex-pected it today.

"Abby wanted to tell you. It was I who asked her not to do so."

"What right did you have to make such a request?" she cried.

"You were mourning the loss of your son. I didn't want you to have to mourn the loss of his child as well."

She rolled her eyes, showing him that she wasn't grateful for that kindness. "Did you ever intend to tell me?"

"Yes, I promised to explain everything before you began work on the christening gown." He glanced at the fabric on the settee, realizing he'd been too late. Abby was probably wondering why he hadn't already spoken to his mother.

Another promise broken, he thought, recalling his irate tenant from that morning. A month ago, Morgan had assured the man that the ditch he'd positioned near a field of crops would not overrun its banks. It had.

He sighed. "I planned to discuss the matter with you last night, but you didn't come down for dinner. This morning, a crisis pulled me away before we could speak."

His mother began pacing. Even the rustling of her black skirts sounded furious. "I don't know what to say. How could you keep this from me? How could Jasper? To think, he married a ruined woman and willingly gave his name to someone else's child! Why would he do such a thing?"

Morgan stiffened. What had his mother said to Abby, exactly? If she was this irate, it couldn't have been kind. Why had Abby not waited for him?

"Did you allow her to explain?" he asked.

"I heard enough. To think how I blathered on about that child and ordered fabric for a christening gown and quilts. I feel ill just thinking about it."

"She was ravished, Mother," Morgan said bluntly. He didn't care if she thought him vulgar. She needed to know the facts.

"Yes, by a man she encouraged."

The coldness of the statement struck a nerve in Morgan. Apparently, Abby had been permitted to explain at least some of her story. It had just fallen on stubborn, unfeeling ears. "A mild flirtation or a chaste kiss does not grant a man permission to take advantage of a woman. For months, she attempted to break the connection."

"I realize that," said his mother. "But she was wrong to encourage his advances at all—she, a gentlewoman!"

"She was naive and lonely. Did you not kiss another man before Father?"

It was the wrong question to ask. The look she cast him was nothing short of indignant. "How dare you suggest such a thing? I most certainly did not."

Morgan ought to have assumed as much. His mother had been born proper. She'd probably never deviated from that course her entire life, other than to play a harmless game of shuttlecock with him once. She'd always behaved with utmost decorum and expected the same from others. Perhaps that was one of the reasons Jasper stayed away, if not *the* reason.

"She didn't have a mother to instruct her about proprieties as you did," Morgan said instead.

"She had a governess."

"An old and inadequate governess."

She looked at him sharply. "Why are you defending her?"

"Because I've come to know Abby. She is a good person, Mother. The only thing she could possibly be accused of is naivety. But she learned her lesson in the most vile and despicable way possible and doesn't need to suffer any more for her mistakes. She is more deserving of our compassion than our censure."

"Compassion," his mother scoffed. "It is plain that she has pulled the wool over your eyes as well. Can you not see she has manipulated us? She probably invented that story to gain Jasper's sympathies, and now she's trying to sink her clutches into you as well. Perhaps she already has."

"Enough." Morgan's jaw clenched. His mother was too upset to think rationally, and Morgan would soon lose his temper if he didn't put a stop to this.

He stared at the woman who'd given him life and strove for a calm voice. "Do you recall the bouquets of wildflowers that your maid placed on your bedside table most mornings soon after Jasper's funeral? I spotted Abby carrying in a handful of flowers one day, and when I spied the same posy on your table, I asked your maid about them. She said that nearly every morning, Abby rose early to gather some blooms for your breakfast tray, then asked the servants to keep her part in it to themselves.

"Does that sound like the workings of a conniving and manipulative woman? You are hurt, and you are speaking in anger. But you've come to know Abby as well. Do you truly believe her capable of lying to us—she, who has brought so much joy into this house and shows the same kindness to all, regardless of station? I admire her, the servants admire her, and up until this morning, you did as well."

His mother did not take the chastisement well. She glared at him before spinning around and putting her back to him again. "Perhaps we should continue this conversation another time."

"I couldn't agree more." Morgan strode from the room. At the top of the stairs, he hesitated, peering down the hall in the direction of Abby's bedchamber. Should he go to her now and explain why he hadn't followed through on his promise, or would it be better to wait?

After his confrontation with his mother, he decided the latter.

Unfortunately, neither Abby nor his mother made an appearance at dinner. Morgan ate alone and sipped his port in silence, staring out the window into the darkness. After a time, he took himself off to bed.

AS SOON AS the sun appeared over the horizon, Morgan dressed and went down to breakfast, intending to wait for Abby in the parlor. To his surprise, he discovered her in the great hall, dressed in a black linen bonnet and matching redingote that didn't quite button over her midsection. His mother's castoffs. She was tucking something that looked like a letter under a vase while two footmen carried a large trunk from the house.

She's leaving.

A chill washed over him, and he trotted down the last few steps.

"Going somewhere, Abby?" he asked, mentally cursing himself for not seeking her out yesterday afternoon. If he had, would they be here now?

She picked up her pair of gloves and faced him with a sad smile. "For now, to Lord and Lady Knave's country estate in Lynfield. After my confinement, I hope to find a small cottage somewhere that will meet my needs."

"This is your home," Morgan insisted. "Don't go."

Another sad smile. "I should have left weeks ago, but I am glad I didn't. I shall always remember my time here with fondness—you, especially. Thank you for your many kindnesses and understanding. Please thank your mother for me as well."

So formal and detached, as though they were nothing more than acquaintances. "Abby, please—"

"I was going to leave this for you, but now that you are here . . ." She picked up the letter that she'd tucked under the vase and held it out to him. When he didn't take it right away, she set it back on the table and added quietly, "Take care, Brigston."

This felt wrong, so horribly wrong, but he knew there was nothing he could say or do to make her stay. The determination in her expression told him that much.

"Will you allow me to drive you to the stage?"

She shook her head. "Your coachman is already waiting to take me. Let's not prolong the inevitable."

The footmen returned for her second trunk, and Morgan waited impatiently for them to carry it from the house. Then he pushed the door closed with one hand and took hold of her hand with the other. "I never got the opportunity to tell her, Abby," he said. "I planned to, I swear I did, but she didn't come down to dinner, and the next morning I was called away for an emergency."

She gave his hand a squeeze. "It should have been me who told her anyhow. It was my burden to share."

"Will you be all right?" he blurted, not willing to relinquish her hand just yet.

She touched her stomach with her free hand and managed a smile. "I already am. I have a child I'll soon meet and dear friends to help me through it. You needn't worry about me any longer."

I can't help it, he wanted to say, but he held the words back, knowing they would only make this harder.

Could it be any harder?

Brigston closed the distance between them and enfolded her in his arms. She stiffened at first but soon relaxed against him, resting the brim of her bonnet against his chest and clutching the lapels of his coat in her fists. He breathed in the familiar scent of apples and committed the feel of her to his memory. When he heard footsteps approach from down the hall, he dropped a kiss on her cheek and croaked, "Goodbye, Abby."

She looked up at him, her blue eyes sparkling with unshed tears. "Goodbye," she whispered before she tore herself away and strode out the door. In no time at all, she was in the coach and driving away.

Every muscle in Morgan's body tensed with the desire to race after the carriage and beg her to marry him. He hated letting her go. He hated duty and honor and responsibility. He hated his title and station. And he hated the law.

"Is there something I can do for you, my lord?" Smithson asked from below. He'd been overseeing Abby's departure and was now returning to the house.

"No." Morgan pulled himself together and walked back inside. As he passed by the side table, he grabbed the letter Abby left before seeking the solace of his study.

He sat at the desk, staring at his name in bold script. The handwriting wasn't the finest he'd ever seen, but it reminded him of her—unrefined, imperfect, kind, loveable Abby.

When he could stand it no longer, he tore open the seal.

Brigston, my friend,

I will not refer to you as my brother because I do not think of you in that way. Someday, I hope to be able to look upon you and not yearn for the impossible, but for now, I must go in a different direction.

Bless you for helping me to smile once again, for giving me the means to live independently, and for understanding my plight. You cannot know how much your friendship has meant to me.

All my gratitude and love,
Abby

Brigston clenched his fingers around the letter and fought the emotion threatening to consume him. He'd always known it would be hard to say goodbye to Abby. He just never realized how hard.

FOURTEEN

ABBY ARRIVED IN the village of Lynfield feeling like she'd been thrown from a horse. Every bit of her ached, even her feet, which was odd since she hadn't used them much at all. She stepped from the airless, foul-smelling coach into a bleak afternoon. A gust of wind swept through her thin, black redingote, chilling her instantly. She inhaled and listened, but there was no smell of the sea or lapping of the waves here.

She followed the other travelers into a bedraggled inn that smelled only marginally better than the coach. Much to her relief, she was ushered into a private parlor where she found Lord and Lady Knave waiting for her.

"Abby!" Prudence saw her first and rushed to embrace her. "How good it is to see you. I was worried I'd have to wait until the middle of the season, and that wouldn't do at all. I'm beyond thrilled that you have come to stay with us again. It feels as though part of our family has returned."

Abby couldn't have asked for a warmer welcome, not that she was surprised. Prudence had always treated her like family.

Abby took a seat on a comfortable chair and leaned back. It felt good to have space to herself and less stuffy air to breathe. She wanted to drag another chair over, kick off her shoes, and prop up her feet, but that kind of relaxation would have to wait until she was tucked away in her bedchamber at Radbourne Abby, and only after a long soak.

A bath. How heavenly that sounded.

Abby considered the couple across from her with fondness. How well they looked together— Prudence, with her silky dark locks and chocolate eyes, and Knave, with his blue eyes, chestnut hair, and devilish smile. Both handsome, both happy. Theirs had been a tale for a romance novel, the sort of books Prudence enjoyed writing.

"How is Sophia?" Abby asked, inquiring after Prudence's sister.

Her friend's smile wilted into a frown. "The same, I'm afraid."

Abby laughed. "Isn't that a good thing? Sophia has always been kind and cheerful. Surely you wouldn't want her to change."

"By *the same,*" inserted Knave with a wry grin, "she means that Sophia is still unmarried."

Abby assumed as much. Prudence had always been a matchmaker at heart. The fact that Sophia had made it through an entire London season unattached was probably the bane of her sister's existence. She'd been so sure she would find the perfect match for Sophia.

"We were sorry to hear about Lord Jasper," said Knave with a look of sympathy. "I did not know him well, but he seemed like a good man."

Prudence nodded her agreement, and although her expression contained the same sympathy, questions swarmed in her eyes. Abby couldn't blame her. Prudence still didn't know why Abby had eloped or what had occurred that horrible night of the ball. Over the past several months, she'd begun many letters to her friend, only to crumple and toss them into the fire. Abby finally realized she could never explain in a letter. She needed to do it in person, only not here at a busy inn with a servant lingering in the corner. There would be time for a long chat later, preferably when Sophia was present.

"Tell me," said Abby with forced brightness, "is Sophia still working with animals?"

"Yes," said Prudence with an eye roll. "Word of her talent has spread, and people bring their troubled animals from all over Oxfordshire. It's ridiculous. One man even arrived with a goat tied to his gig. Can you believe it? He complained that the wretched beast would eat all his wife's dahlias, and he wanted Sophia to fix the problem."

Abby chuckled. "What did she say?"

"She reminded him that goats are known to eat flowers, or anything, really, and that if he didn't want the animal dining on his wife's garden he should erect a fence around either the goat or the flowers."

"Did she manage a straight face?"

"Almost entirely," said Prudence, "though I did see her lips twitch a time or two when the man asked if there was something she could do to change the goat's appetite. Poor man. He drove for hours only to be disappointed that my sister could not charm his goat."

"Prudence thinks she should start requiring a fee for her services," said Knave.

"She never would," added his wife. "But I find it ludicrous that people expect her to spend so much of her time fixing their animals without any sort of compensation, although one man did attempt to thank her with a marriage proposal." Prudence made a face to show what she'd thought of that. "He was bald, portly, and twice her age. But he had a great many problematic animals and was certain a union between them would benefit both parties."

"How would it have benefited Sophia, exactly?" asked Abby.

"He could provide all the animals she could ever want to help," said Knave dryly.

In that moment Abby knew she'd come to the right place. She'd missed her friends, their humor, their laughter, and the wonderful way they viewed the world. If she was going to make it through the next several months with her optimism intact, she would need them at her side.

I have been blessed, she thought.

"If those are the sorts of proposals she's receiving, I can understand why she has not married," said Abby.

"Not for lack of us trying." Worried lines appeared across Prudence's brow. She probably still held herself to blame for stealing the affections of her sister's intended the previous year. Lord Knave had been meant to marry Sophia so they might join the two family's properties together, but when he fell in love with Prudence instead, it upset those plans. Prudence wouldn't rest until she saw her sister as happily situated.

"Did she receive no offers last season?" asked Abby. From what she could remember, Sophia had several men buzzing around her. Abby had been certain at least one of them would come up to scratch.

"Yes, but she didn't trust any of them to be sincere in their affections," said Prudence. "And frankly, neither did I. They all valued her dowry more than her."

"I can understand that feeling." Abby had also gone to London with a sizable dowry, and she'd felt that same concern with a number of men. In a way, Prudence had been lucky not to be an heiress. She never had a reason to question

Lord Knave's sincerity, not that anyone would question it. One only had to see the pair look at each other to know they were in love.

Abby caught Prudence watching her again—her expression thoughtful, curious . . . worried. It was only a matter of time before the questioning began.

She leaned forward and clutched her friend's hand. "We shall talk after we return to Radbourne Abbey. Perhaps we can stop and collect Sophia from Talford Hall on our way?"

Prudence brightened and nodded. "I think we can arrange that. Shall we be off then?" she asked her husband.

"Now? The refreshment we ordered has not yet arrived."

Prudence waved her hand dismissively. "The tea at the Abbey will taste infinitely better."

Knave cast his wife a look of forbearance, tossed some coins on the table, and called for the carriage. As they drove from the innyard, Abby wondered if there would ever be a place she would permanently call home.

FIFTEEN

THE DAYS BECAME shorter and chillier as October trickled into November and November became December. Each morning, rain or shine, wind or still, Morgan cantered his horse down the same stretch of beach where he'd stumbled upon Abby.

Anyone who knew the extent of his feelings might call him mad for intentionally taking a route that made him think of her. He often wondered the same, but he'd remind himself that thinking and speaking of Jasper had eased the loss of his brother, and so he continued riding to the beach and thinking of her.

Unfortunately, it only made him miss her more. He wanted to see her walking, or even riding. He wanted to offer his elbow and walk with her, hear her laugh, see her smile, and feel the delights of her embrace.

He and his mother were now in half-mourning, but other than the color of their clothes, not much had changed. They still didn't attend soirées or dances, and the Christmas Eve party they had hosted every year since Morgan could remember, with the exception of the year his father had died, had not been discussed. Morgan could only assume his mother had no plans to host it this year either.

Friends called on them and invitations arrived almost weekly, but none had been accepted. Apparently, his mother had no wish to socialize, and Morgan didn't either. But he needed to do *something*. With his estate's renovations on hold, he spent too much time thinking about Abby. What was she doing? How was she faring? When would her child arrive?

Out of desperation, he accepted an invitation to a winter's ball. His mother didn't want to accompany him, so he went alone. The moment he entered the ballroom, however, all he could think about was the day he and Abby had played shuttlecock. He even glanced up at the chandelier, hoping to see a racket and a shuttlecock hanging there. It was ludicrous. He forced himself through a dance or two, a few discussions with some neighbors, and an introduction to a young, pretty chit, but she didn't make him smile, laugh, or yearn for more. As soon as he could, Morgan made his excuses and went out into the cold, December night.

This would never do. He needed to get his mind off Abby or he'd go mad.

Perhaps he already had.

By the time Christmas Eve arrived, Morgan knew he couldn't stay at Oakley any longer. He needed a change, he needed distance, and he needed air to breathe that didn't always seem to smell like apples. Parliament wouldn't be back in session for over a month, but it might be better if he left for London early and found something there to preoccupy him. His family's townhouse held precious few memories of Abby.

As he and his mother dined on Yorkshire Christmas pie, Morgan decided to broach the subject. He set down his fork, rested his elbows on the table, and interlocked his fingers under his chin.

"I was thinking we should go to London after the first of the year."

Her fork hovered over her plate as she considered him. Though she still appeared worn, her lavender gown gave her complexion some color, and she'd returned to her more fashionable hair styles, which softened her features.

"So soon?" she asked.

"I need a change. I need to be somewhere that . . ." *doesn't constantly remind me of Abby.* "Somewhere else."

His mother dismissed the servants in the room, then slowly lowered her fork to her plate and her gaze with it. "I miss her, too."

Her confession surprised Morgan. She hadn't spoken of Abby since she'd left. Then again, she rarely spoke of those she missed, so perhaps that should have given him some indication as to her feelings. Perhaps he'd been too busy blaming her to take note of that.

"It's become as dull as dishwater around here, hasn't it?" she asked.

"It's . . . quieter." *Lonelier,* he added to himself. Interesting how loneliness had never bothered him before.

"I finished the christening gown," she said. "I'm not sure why, but I did. Now I'm at a loss as to what to do with it. Should I send it to her? Should I put it away with Jasper's old things? I feel like that child should be mine, yet it isn't. How silly is that?"

"It *is* yours," said Morgan. "Jasper made it so when he married Abby. Do you not see? The best parts of him live on in her. She's cheerful and amusing, and her memories of Jasper are more generous than mine. She saw the good in him and reminded me of it as well. The child she now carries may not be of your flesh and blood, but if she raises him as Jasper's son, there will be a part of him in that boy even if they don't share a likeness."

"Boy?" His mother's smile vanished, and she leaned forward. "Have you been in communication with her? Has the child arrived early?"

Morgan berated himself for his slip of the tongue. He wanted the child to be a boy so badly he'd begun to think of it as such.

"I didn't mean to say that," he said, tossing his napkin on the table.

His mother watched him closely for a few moments before speaking. "A boy would become your heir."

She had always been too perceptive. "Yes."

Silence followed—a long, accusatory silence where Morgan felt as though he were on trial and would soon be found guilty.

"You love her." It was a statement, not a question, so Morgan didn't bother answering. She had to see the truth in his eyes.

His mother nodded slowly, worriedly.

Morgan wanted to groan. Was he really considering a forbidden marriage and risking his family's holdings? He had always been responsible and duty-bound, but now . . . now he didn't care as much.

"You'd have to marry in a parish where you are not known," she said.

"I know."

"Your marriage could be voided, your future children declared illegitimate."

"Only if someone contests it."

"Are you willing to take that chance, to live with that concern the rest of your life?"

Morgan pushed his plate aside and massaged his temples with one hand, hating the black mood that threatened to suffocate him. "I don't know," he finally said.

If only Jasper hadn't married her. If only Morgan had made more of an effort socially and met her first. If only he'd been the one to escort her to Vauxhall Gardens. That filthy cur wouldn't have had the opportunity to defile her. Morgan wouldn't have been able to keep his eyes off her the entire evening. He would have been but a few steps behind and could have protected her.

Why weren't you there, Jasper? Why didn't you see him?

Morgan dropped his head into his hands with a groan. "I know I should look elsewhere for a wife, but . . ." He shook his head, unable to finish. His mother knew what he was thinking. How could she not? Her eyes mirrored the worry and fear he felt.

She removed the napkin from her lap and tossed it onto the table. "I don't know what the answer is, Morgan, but I think you are correct in one thing. We should go to London after the first of the year. Perhaps the foul-smelling air will clear our senses."

He could only pray she was right.

SIXTEEN

ABBY BLINKED AT the light filtering through the crack in her drapes with relief. Good. Morning had finally come. One more long and tedious night was behind her, and according to her doctor, she should only have about a handful more to go.

She struggled to prop herself up, her large belly making it a chore. Everywhere hurt. Her back was the worst, with her legs and feet not far behind. She lifted the covers and frowned at her ever-fattening ankles. The doctor assured her it was normal, but they didn't look normal to her, and she certainly didn't feel normal. She felt miserable.

It was no wonder women hid themselves away during this wretched time.

She stretched her arms high overhead, trying to work out some of the aches in her shoulders. When she dropped them back down, her fingers grazed something that crinkled. She looked over to see the package that had arrived yesterday. Inside, she'd found a white muslin christening gown, with perfect stitches, intricate embroidery, and delicate lace. There had been no card or note enclosed, only the gown.

Abby still didn't know what to make of it. Was it an

apology? A peace offering? A goodbye? Or was it merely Lady Brigston's way of saying, *I purchased this fabric for a christening gown for your child. You may as well put it to use since I have no need of it.*

"Would it have been so hard to include a note?" Abby asked to no one in particular. She sighed and rang for her maid, wishing for all the world that Brigston would appear on the doorstep. He would explain. He would bolster her spirits. He would make her smile and forget her discomfort.

How easy it was to envision him lying here next to her with his hand on her stomach, chuckling every time her child's foot or elbow protruded.

She drew in a breath and reaffirmed her resolve not to think about him for at least one day.

Beginning now.

"I hold you mostly to blame for the way I feel," she said, tapping on her stomach. In response, the baby's foot or elbow dug into her, producing a lump on her midsection.

"You have to be a boy," she said. "A girl wouldn't be nearly as troublesome." When something jabbed at her stomach again, Abby smiled. Apparently her little one was ready for morning as well.

With the help of Evie, Abby dressed and tried to ignore her reflection in the looking glass. One more month, and she could stop wearing black. She might have felt guilty for such selfish thoughts, but Jasper wouldn't have liked seeing her in this color either.

She could almost hear him say, *You should have mourned wearing the color of a blue sky on a clear day as a tribute to me. I would have liked that infinitely better.*

Me too, thought Abby, deciding that the first gown she'd order out of mourning would be a pale blue in honor of her late husband.

She found Prudence and Sophia in the drawing room, sipping tea. Sophia came to call most mornings, hoping for news of the babe. Prudence's dog, Scamp, was curled up on her lap, enjoying a nice rub.

"Any pains yet?" Prudence asked when she spied Abby.

Abby shook her head, then smiled when Prudence clucked in disappointment.

Sophia rolled her eyes, her red ringlets bouncing softly against her cheeks. "You sound as though you'd like her to be in pain, Pru."

"I would," she said, making Abby laugh.

"I would as well," said Abby. "If that's what it will take to breathe deeply again, I shall gladly submit to it. Well, perhaps not too gladly."

Prudence patted the settee at her side. "Come join us. We were just discussing how soon the doctor will allow you to go with us to London."

Abby stifled a yawn as she sank down next to her friend. She couldn't remember what it felt like to not be tired. "Will you never give up?"

"Never."

Whether or not Abby would go with them to London had been a highly debated discussion over the past few months. Prudence and Sophia wanted her to travel with them, and Abby insisted that as soon as she recovered, she should begin her search for a cottage.

Over the passing months, however, Abby's convictions grew weaker and weaker. Oh, she needed to move on with her life and locating a cottage would be the next step, but now that she'd grown accustomed to the companionship, friendship, and support of her two friends, she was loathe to give that up. The moment she started thinking that the season's end might be a better time to make the transition, she knew she was going to relent. Prudence was too stubborn and her arguments too alluring.

It didn't help that Brigston would be in London as well. He might already be there, as parliament would open again in a few days. How Abby longed to see him again, if only from a distance. She shouldn't long for it, but she did. It was the most vexing aspect of being human.

"Your energies would be better spent helping me locate a cottage," said Abby, not ready to give Prudence the satisfaction of winning the argument just yet.

As always, her friend was ready to counter. She grinned slyly. "If you come to London with us, perhaps you won't need a cottage in the end."

Abby didn't appreciate the implication. In fact, it was the only aspect of going to London that still made her hesitate. Prudence would do her best to find Abby a new husband, even though Abby had pointed out a number of times that she would still be in mourning and had no interest in marrying again anytime soon. Now that she knew what it felt like to really connect with someone, she could never settle for anything less.

Abby shifted positions on the settee, hoping to alleviate some of the pain in her lower back. "How about a compromise, Pru?" she suggested.

Both Prudence and her dog seemed to perk up at this.

"If I agree to go with you to London, you must agree to be only my friend, not my matchmaker."

Prudence frowned, obviously not liking that particular compromise. Sophia, on the other hand, thought it a great plan.

"That's brilliant, Abby," she said. "Why didn't I think to suggest the same?"

"Because you are going to London whether you like it or not," said Prudence to her sister.

"Perhaps I should contract rheumatic fever again so that I might stay home," Sophia teased, her hazel eyes twinkling.

"Don't even jest about such things," said her sister. "You are not allowed to become that ill ever again. Understood?"

"Only if you promise not to—"

"Oh, for goodness' sake," said Prudence crossly. "I shall see you both happily situated one day, and that is that."

Abby should have known her friend would never capitulate. Meddling was too ingrained in her, especially when it came to love. She was a romantic at heart and always would be, and she would not rest until her sister and friend found their own Lord Knaves.

Abby shifted again, wishing she could find a position that offered some comfort. Perhaps a pillow would help? She spotted one on the floor near her feet and leaned to the side to snag it, but something strange happened. She felt a small pop inside of her, like a bubble that had been poked, followed by a rush of warm liquid between her legs. It took her a moment to realize what had occurred—the doctor had warned something of this nature could happen—but she still felt unprepared. She froze, excitement and fear rippling through her like rivulets in the sea.

It was time.

She looked at her friend and prayed the quiver in her voice would not give her away. "What about a wager instead, Pru? If the babe arrives by the day's end, you must promise to cease your matchmaking efforts for both Sophia *and* me."

Prudence's expression became suspicious, but she eventually nodded. "Only if *you* agree that if the child does not come today, you will allow me to matchmake to my heart's content."

Abby had no idea how long it took for a babe to arrive beyond this point, but it was still early in the day. Surely it would come before nightfall. Her stomach cramped ever so slightly—another sign the doctor had told her to expect when the time of delivery neared.

"Agreed," Abby said quickly. "Now, if you'd be so kind as to send for the doctor, Sophia, I'd be most grateful. And Pru, would you help me to my room, please? I should like to escape the drawing room before I leave a larger puddle on your furniture."

A moment of stunned silence followed this pronouncement before the sisters became a flurry of excitement. Sophia practically ran from the room, presumably to send for the doctor, and Prudence shouted for someone to assist her. A footman came rushing in, and the two helped Abby back to her room. Not long after that, the cramping began to worsen.

By the time the doctor arrived, Abby decided that she'd rather remain swollen and short of breath than suffer through the pain of childbirth. Her lower back screamed in agony every time a pain came on, and the disobliging doctor said she had a ways to go yet.

Much to her torment, the child did not arrive until the wee hours of the following morning. By that point, Abby was too exhausted to care about her agreement with Prudence. All she wanted to do was see her baby and sleep.

The doctor gently wrapped a crying, wriggly babe in a quilt and laid it in Abby's arms, saying quietly, "Congratulations, Lady Jasper. You have a daughter."

Her heart plummeted at the news, but one look at her beautiful baby girl, and Abby adored her instantly. So tiny, innocent, and precious.

How could she possibly regret such a gift?

SEVENTEEN

FOUR COACHES WERE required to carry the party from Lynfield to London. Prudence and Knave rode with Prudence's parents, Mr. and Mrs. Gifford, while Abby sat with her baby, lady's maid, nurse, and Sophia. The last two carriages held the other ladies' maids and valets. Knave's father, Lord Bradden, was recovering from a bout of pneumonia, so he and Lady Bradden had chosen to remain at home for the season.

Only a few hours into their journey, Abby worried that Sophia regretted her decision to accompany her. Little Anne had been crying for nearly an hour. She'd been passed from Abby to the nurse to her lady's maid and back to Abby, but no amount of cooing or jostling would shush her.

"What the devil is the matter, Anne?" Abby finally spoke her frustration. "You've been fed, changed, and coddled. We've even tried singing to you, but you don't seem to care for that either. So what is it? Are you hoping to ride with our coachman? Is that it? Because I'm nearly ready to put you up with him."

Nurse Lovell stared at her in alarm while Sophia chuckled and held out her arms. "Let me have a go."

Abby felt some remorse handing over a screaming child,

but if Sophia could soothe distraught animals, perhaps she could soothe a babe as well. Abby could only pray that would be the case. They were probably all praying, even the coachman, who could undoubtedly hear Anne's wails over the crunch of pebbles on the road.

It took Sophia all of five minutes to get her asleep.

"However did you do that?" Abby asked in awe.

"You're a wonder, Miss," added the nurse, her round face a mixture of amazement and relief. She wiped away the perspiration from her forehead with her sleeve and relaxed against the back of the cushions. It was a chilly, March morning, but with five bodies inside the coach and warm bricks near their feet, they were all cozy.

"She was simply tired," said Sophia in her unassuming way. "She would have probably fallen asleep in your arms as well, given a few more minutes."

Abby seriously doubted that. She nearly asked Sophia if she'd be willing to instruct her nurse how to soothe babies, but she figured the woman might take offense to that. Nurse Lovell was a dear, and seemed to genuinely adore Anne, but whenever the child became upset, which was quite often, so did the nurse. It was something Abby hoped would subside in time.

Not long after Anne quieted, Evie and Nurse Lovell nodded off as well. Abby could hardly blame them. It had been a trying morning, and she longed to join them, but she couldn't bring herself to do so while Sophia cared for her child.

"It seems you have a knack for children as well as animals," said Abby softly, not wanting to wake Anne.

Sophia grinned. "If that's the case, it's a shame I may never have any of my own." No matter her circumstances, she always maintained her sense of humor—something Abby admired about her.

"I'll just have to be the doting aunt to little Anne and Prudence's future children. Such a trial that will be." She snuggled Anne closer and kissed her cheek, looking perfectly happy.

Abby couldn't resist resting her head against the side of the coach. She'd removed her bonnet hours ago and could feel her hair frizz around her face. "I would love that above all things, Soph, but you know as well as I that Prudence would never stand for it. She will see you married before the season is out, mark my words."

"You said that same thing at the beginning of last season as well, yet here I am, still unattached."

Abby studied her friend's profile. Her kind smile, bright eyes, and hair a ghastly shade of red. Few would call Sophia a beauty, but she *was* beautiful. She just needed to find someone who could look beyond her freckles and wide-set eyes. Abby hoped she would find such a man one day. If anyone deserved marital bliss, it was her friend.

Abby looked out the window at the rolling hills that would soon be covered in colorful blossoms and shades of green. Oxfordshire was lovely in the spring. It was her favorite time of year.

"You, on the other hand, will have no problem securing a husband," said Sophia. "You were one of the most sought after debutantes last season, and now you're returning as a stunning, independent widow. The men are going to flock about you."

Abby didn't want men to flock about her. She only wanted one. "I am still in half mourning and have no interest in marrying again anytime soon."

Sophia tilted her head, her expression contemplative and curious. "Did you love Lord Jasper? I know he rescued you and this little one, so he certainly earned your regard in that respect, but . . . did you love him? You need not answer if you'd rather not."

Abby hesitated. She'd been open with her friends about the events leading up to her marriage, but she'd done so without betraying her feelings for Jasper or his brother. They hadn't prodded her for more, at least not until now, though Sophia could never be accused of prying.

There was a reason Abby hadn't been forthcoming with her feelings for Brigston. If Prudence ever learned that her closest friend had already lost her heart, she'd stop at nothing to get them together. The law, the risks, his title and obligations—Prudence would disregard it all, or at least attempt to do so, just as Abby had done once upon a time.

Sophia, on the other hand, was not like her sister. She could be counted upon not to interfere, and she could be trusted to keep this conversation between them.

"I did love Jasper," Abby admitted, "but not in the way Prudence believes a wife should love her husband, although I desperately wish I could have. He saved me and Anne from a fate worse than death, only to lose his life in the bargain. How could I not love him for that? I will always honor his memory, I'll raise Anne to know the sort of man her father was, and I will fully mourn his death. But if I am being completely honest, I have since lost my heart to another."

Sophia's eyes widened in surprise. She glanced briefly at the two servants, probably to assure herself they were still asleep, before looking back at Abby.

"Who?" She asked the question so quietly that Abby read her lips more than heard the words.

Abby swallowed, despising the emotion threatening to rise within her. It had been over five months since she'd seen or spoken of him out loud. Would she never move beyond this?

"A man I can never have," said Abby woodenly. "Jasper's brother and now mine."

EIGHTEEN

THE HACKNEY HIT a rut, jostling Morgan as he returned to his townhouse after a lengthy parliament session, which included a heated debate about the need for improved working conditions in cotton mills, particularly with regard to the children. It had begun at four o'clock that afternoon and lasted nearly six hours.

He couldn't fathom why anyone would oppose passing a law that prevented mills from working children more than ten hours a day, but there had been plenty of opposition. It made him ill just picturing children toiling for that long, their hands raw, bodies weary, and lungs filled with cotton. He'd wanted to demand that children not be allowed to work at all, but families relied on that income, and if their children ceased working, they ceased eating. So he'd sided with those in favor of reducing the hours and bettering the conditions as much as possible.

Discussions like this took everything out of him. Sometimes he wondered how long he could continue trying to promote change when change was so slow to happen. But ignoring the problems, like many of his peers preferred to do, wasn't an option for him. Despite the exhaustion and frustration, Morgan would continue to fight for those who could not fight for themselves.

The hackney pulled to a stop in front of his townhouse on Brooks Street in Mayfair. As he looked up at the impressive, four-story edifice, he wondered, not for the first time, why he had so much while others had nothing. It was that feeling of guilt that carried him to London each season for the interminable parliament sessions.

He exited the hackney, wanting nothing more than to relax with a strong drink and a book, but alas, he'd promised his mother they'd attend Lady Campshire's soirée that evening. They were going to be fashionably late, as was usual after a parliament session, but that would not matter to his mother. She only wanted to forget her struggles for a time among the whirl of the ton.

Morgan carried himself up to his room, where he washed the grime and sweat from his body in a quick bath. He dressed in a manner befitting a marquess and mentally prepared himself for hours of tedious conversation. Lady Campshire's parties were always a crush.

He tried his best to dismiss the harrowing day from his mind as he went to collect his mother, who'd waited patiently in the drawing room. Now that she was officially out of mourning, she wore a smart sapphire gown and appeared almost like her old, radiant self. It was good to see, and by the time they arrived at the soirée, his mood had lifted, as had his appetite. He hoped they hadn't missed dinner because he was suddenly ravenous.

"Do try to be sociable this evening," said his mother as they ascended the stairs to the house.

"I'm always sociable," answered Morgan. Coming to London early had been the right decision even though there had been precious few social activities in the beginning. The change of scenery had done them both good.

"I disagree," said his mother. "You speak only to those

you wish to speak with and ignore all others, looking either bored or aloof."

"I often *am* bored."

"That may be, but you don't have to look it."

They crossed over the threshold into the house, and Morgan helped her with her coat. "If it would please you, I shall do my utmost to be congenial, charming, and engaged this evening. But if anyone should ask me which neckcloth looks more distinguished or what I think about Sally Jersey's new coiffure, I shall reciprocate by recounting the details of today's discussion in the House of Lords. If I cannot appear bored, I shall be boring."

They approached their hostess, and his mother offered her a wide smile. "Lady Campshire, how lovely you look this evening."

And so it began. Morgan took the lady's hand and bowed over it, offering a charming and obligatory lie. "Every time we meet, you look younger than the last. Pray tell, what is your secret?"

Lady Campshire simpered and smiled and flirtatiously tapped his shoulder with her fan. "What nonsense, my lord."

Utter nonsense, he agreed inwardly. Outwardly, he said, "Not at all."

This earned him a delighted titter from his hostess, along with a look from his mother that said, *You're doing it a bit too brown.*

He had to stifle his answering smile and took his mother by the elbow instead, planning to lead her into the room, but Lady Campshire waylaid him with a hand on his arm.

"Tell me, Lord Brigston, why is it that you and your mother accepted my invitation for this evening while your sister did not?"

Morgan stiffened and looked back at her. "Sister?"

"Lady Jasper, of course. Who else would I be referring to?" She tittered again.

"Lady Jasper is not in London."

Her eyes widened in a gleeful way, as though she was happy to share a juicy bit of gossip. "She arrived last week with Lord and Lady Knave. I thought you, of all people, would have been made aware. I hear her daughter is quite the angel."

Abby? Here? In London? Morgan's heart seemed to stop abruptly before starting again with a stutter. She'd had a girl. *No.*

He tried not to show an outward reaction but all he could think was, *A girl.* The words thudded through his mind like the pounding of a gavel in parliament. His heir was still his mangy cousin, Markus.

His mother came to his rescue, leaning across him with a ready fib. "What he means to say is that we were not aware she had arrived so soon. We expected her next week. And the child *is* an angel. You must stop by and see for yourself sometime. Oh, look, here's Mr. and Mrs. Linton. How wonderful to see you both." His mother effectively redirected Lady Campshire's attention to the next guests in line, allowing her and Morgan to get away.

Morgan followed, feeling like he'd just taken a surprise jab to the face.

Lady Campshire had to be mistaken. She couldn't possibly know with certainty that—

Why did his mother not appear more surprised? He waited for her to finish greeting someone before pulling her aside. "Did you know?"

"I only learned about it this afternoon," she said.

"And you didn't see fit to tell me?" The moment the question came out, he heard his own hypocrisy. She'd asked him a similar question not so long ago.

Under her breath, she said, "I was hoping we could make it through this evening before I broke the news. I'd rather you appear bored than brooding." She smiled and nodded at another acquaintance before giving him a stern look. "We will discuss this later."

His mother had been right to worry about his reaction. For the remainder of the evening Morgan spoke only when spoken to and kept his responses short and clipped. By the time his mother pronounced she was ready to depart, he stood alone in a corner, having driven away even the most gregarious members of the ton.

"IF YOU THINK Mr. Wallace is a good fit for Sophia, we should put Mr. Rend in her path as well," said Knave in a wry voice to his wife. He, Abby, and Prudence were seated in the drawing room during their at home hours, awaiting callers. Sophia had gone with her mother for a fitting at the modiste, and Mr. Gifford had escaped to White's, leaving Abby and Knave to rein in Prudence's matchmaking attempts.

So far, it wasn't working.

Prudence made a face, and Abby laughed, enjoying their banter.

"Mr. Rend is a dreadful bore," said Prudence.

"As is Mr. Wallace," answered her husband.

"But he loves animals, and Sophia seemed to enjoy her discussion with him at the musicale last evening."

Abby grimaced when she thought of the previous night. The myriad of musical numbers, many of which were on par with her own mediocre talents, had dragged on and on. It had been a long evening.

Following the performances, their hostess had introduced Abby and Sophia to Mr. Rend and Mr. Wallace. They were good-natured men and attractive enough, but their eyes did not sparkle with humor and they seemed more concerned with flattering the women than making interesting conversation. Abby managed a smile here and there, but as soon as the opportunity arose, she made her escape. Sophia, on the other hand, had been much more gracious.

"I must agree with Knave," said Abby. "Sophia was merely being kind. Mr. Wallace did not engage her interest in the slightest. Didn't you notice how quickly she changed the subject when you asked about him during our ride home?"

Prudence frowned, and Abby hid a smile. Her friend despised being wrong, especially when it came to matters of the heart. She considered herself somewhat of an expert on the subject even though none of her matchmaking efforts had amounted to much.

"Are you certain?" she asked.

"Quite," said Abby and Knave in unison, causing Prudence's frown to deepen.

The butler entered the room, carrying himself in his rigid, posturing way. His mop of gray hair didn't move a smidgeon when he announced, "Lady Brigston to see Lady Jasper."

In an instant, Abby's smile vanished, and she forgot all about the butler. Lady Brigston had come to see her? Why?

She fisted the fabric of her white afternoon dress, contemplating how to tell the butler she was not at home to visitors. Unfortunately, Prudence spoke before Abby could formulate a believable excuse.

"Please show her in, Dodge."

Abby tightened her grip on her skirts as panic tightened

its grip on her. It was a cowardly response, she knew. The woman could do her no harm. But Abby would never forget Lady Brigston's cold, parting words. *I think it would be better for all our sakes if you left Oakley as soon as possible.*

The words had injured Abby more than she'd ever admit out loud. Had Lady Brigston come to ask Abby to leave London as well? If so, she wouldn't do it. She'd come at the invitation of her friends, and she would remain with them.

Lady Brigston walked into the room, looking confident and more vibrant than Abby remembered her. The strain around her eyes had eased, as had the dark circles. She no longer looked like a fragile waif. Even her brown hair seemed to shine with more luster.

"Lord and Lady Knave, a pleasure," she greeted. "And Abby, it is wonderful to see you again. Her gaze lingered on her daughter-in-law, no doubt to assess her the way Abby had just done. "You look lovely, my dear."

Abby's mouth suddenly felt as though it had been filled with cotton. The last thing she'd expected from this woman was warmth or kindness. Did she mean it?

"Do join us," said Knave. He was standing next to his wife, gesturing to the chair at Abby's side. Lady Brigston sat down and smiled as though all was perfectly normal when it felt anything but.

When Abby finally collected her voice, she said the only thing that came to mind. "This is a surprise, my lady."

"A pleasant surprise," Prudence added, darting a worried look at Abby before smiling at Lady Brigston once more.

"I might say the same about your arrival in London," Lady Brigston said pointedly to Abby.

Abby had to force her lips into a smile, even though it

probably looked as phony as it felt. Did Lady Brigston mean Abby's arrival had been a pleasant surprise or an unpleasant one? If only the people of the ton weren't so adept at masking their true feelings. It could be most unnerving.

"Abby was determined to stay in Lynfield and locate a cottage, but after months of begging, we managed to convince her to join us for another season—and little Anne as well."

Lady Brigston seemed to freeze in place. Her serene expression, her hands in her lap, even her eyes ceased blinking. The only sign she was still breathing was the slight rise and fall of her chest. Was she angry? Offended? Appalled?

"You named your daughter Anne?" she finally asked.

Abby nodded slowly, wondering when she'd become so fearful of this woman. She'd never felt that way about her before. Wary, yes, but not fearful. It was a bizarre reaction. What did she have to lose? Lady Brigston's good opinion? She'd lost that months ago.

Finding her courage, Abby lifted her chin and made her voice sound as confident as possible. "Anne Caroline Campbell, after her two grandmothers." Anne, after Lady Brigston, and Caroline after her own mother.

Her mother-in-law began blinking rapidly, and Abby caught a sheen of moisture in the woman's eyes. Her body nearly sagged in relief. She was happy. Hallelujah.

"May I meet her?" Lady Brigston's voice trembled ever so slightly, and Abby was quick to nod. It was like a wish granted. She'd love nothing more than to introduce her daughter to her only living grandmother.

"Would you like to accompany me to the nursery, or shall I have Nurse Lovell bring her down?"

"The nursery, please." Lady Brigston sounded anxious,

as though she couldn't wait to see her grandchild. Abby could scarce believe it. It all felt too wonderful to be real.

She led the way up to the nursery and entered the room quietly. Nurse Lovell sat dozing in the rocking chair but awoke to the sound of the floor creaking.

The moment she spotted them, she jumped up, glancing at the crib where Anne lay peacefully sleeping. "I didn't mean to fall asleep, my lady. Is there something I can do for you?"

"Not at all," said Abby kindly. Anne had slept fitfully since they'd arrived in London, which made it so Nurse Lovell didn't get much sleep. The poor woman was probably worn to the bone. "Why don't you lie down? We'll look after Anne for a time."

"Oh no, I couldn't," said the nurse. She wasn't a tall woman, but she was large, like a fluffy pillow. Compared to the other rail-thin nurses who had interviewed for the position, Abby thought Anne would be much more comfortable in Nurse Lovell's arms. And she was, for the most part.

Abby laid a hand on the nurse's shoulder. "I know Anne has kept you up many nights, and I'm sorry for it. You must be exhausted. Please go and rest. Anne's grandmother and I will wake you when we're ready to go down."

Nurse Lovell's frame seemed to relax in relief. "If you're sure."

"I'm sure." Abby shooed her into the room adjacent to the nursery.

Lady Brigston walked over to the crib and peered down. Tears sparkled in her eyes as she watched her granddaughter sleep. "She's beautiful," she whispered.

"She's a dear as well, at least some of the time. Nurse Lovell says she has the lungs of an elephant."

Her mother-in-law chuckled softly. "May I hold her?"

"Certainly, but you do so at your own peril. Elephant jokes aside, I wouldn't be surprised if her wails can be heard as far as Scotland."

"I shall take my chances." Lady Brigston lifted the babe from the crib and tucked her to her chest, gently rocking and cooing quietly. Anne stirred but did not awaken.

"You have a magical touch," Abby said, enjoying the sight of her mother-in-law holding her granddaughter. She never would have believed it possible had she not seen it with her own eyes.

The two women settled down, Lady Brigston in the rocking chair and Abby in an armchair by the fireplace. Abby couldn't help but wonder if Brigston would take a liking to Anne as well. He'd look so handsome cuddling her in that rocking chair.

That will never happen.

Abby pushed the image from her mind and cleared her throat. "I haven't thanked you for the christening gown. It was exquisite."

"I'm glad it met with your approval. I should have sent a note, but how does one properly apologize in a letter?" Lady Brigston lifted her gaze to Abby, her forehead creased in consternation. "I was hurt and angry, and reacted in a way I deeply regret. I'm sorry for it."

"You had good reason to be hurt and angry," Abby said. "Jasper and I should have told you straightaway, but he . . ." What was she saying? The last thing Abby wanted to do was place the blame on her late husband. He'd only done what he thought best at the time, and she'd placed her trust in him.

Lady Brigston's eyes twinkled. "He could be quite persuasive, couldn't he?"

"I owed him my life. I would have given him anything."

Except my love, Abby thought shamefully. If only a person could give love to whomever they wished.

"Morgan can be persuasive as well," Lady Brigston added.

It was true. Abby hadn't overridden either brother. "Or perhaps I am too compliant."

"I seriously doubt that." Lady Brigston leaned over to smell the infant, then tenderly placed her cheek against Anne's. "She is so soft. I forgot how small they are. How precious."

Abby said nothing. She only watched, her heart toasty and happy.

"Morgan was right to ask that you keep it from me in the beginning," said his mother. "I needed to be in a better place to weather the news. I only wish I would not have come down so hard on you. Will you forgive an old woman?"

"Only if you forgive me. I would love for Anne to grow up knowing you. Every girl should have at least one doting grandmother."

Lady Brigston seemed to agree with that as well, judging by the brightness in her eyes. "What about you, Abby? Do you have need of a mother?"

Was she offering?

"Yes," said Abby. "Very much so."

Lady Brigston smiled a little and continued rocking Anne. After a few moments, she rested her head against the back of the chair and considered Abby. "I hope you will consider staying with us again, once the season ends. Oakley has been a lonely place since you left."

Abby nearly blurted she would love that above all things, but while she ached to belong to a family, it wasn't that simple. Her feelings for Brigston made it impossible for her to accept.

"As much as I would love to return with you, I need to make a life of my own and live as I see fit. But wherever I make that life, know that you will always be welcome. I'm counting on frequent visits from you."

"Will you visit us as well?"

"I will try." It was the most Abby could promise. If her feelings for Brigston would ever subside, she'd do more than try.

Lady Brigston opened her mouth to say something, but Anne stirred and whimpered a little, so she rocked and coddled her again. "I don't think Anne cared for that answer, Abby. Perhaps you should revisit it."

Abby managed a smile, knowing full well that she hadn't cared for it either.

NINETEEN

MUSIC. VOICES. LAUGHTER. Crystal goblets tinkling. The excited energy in the room mingled with the noises, swirling around Abby and lifting her spirits. Lord and Lady Fernside's ball could officially be declared a success. Abby had rarely seen so many people in one setting before. There was hardly room to dance.

It was good she'd come to London. Here, a person could never feel lonely.

She watched Sophia on the dance floor, walking gracefully through the steps of the minuet with Mr. Wallace. Though she smiled and conversed and executed the steps beautifully, she did not laugh. It was a sure sign he would never do for Sophia. She needed a man who could amuse and interest her. Life would be too difficult without diverting conversations.

Prudence's elbow nudged Abby's arm. "I must concede that you and Knave are right. Mr. Wallace is not lively enough for Sophia, is he?"

"No, but he is a good dancer."

She nodded, her expression pensive. "Why are you not on the floor? I only just saw you speaking with Mr. Egerton. Did he not ask you to stand up with him?"

"He did, but I told him I would not be dancing this evening."

"You cannot be serious."

"I am," said Abby. "If there is a benefit to being a widow, it's that I can do as I please, and tonight, I'd rather watch than be watched. You can try your hardest to dissuade me, but I am not on the hunt for a husband, and I don't plan to be for some time."

Prudence frowned. "I'm beginning to think you and Sophia have joined forces against me. She said the same thing only yesterday."

"You have found us out," said Abby. "We have made a pact to thwart your meddlesome, albeit well-intentioned, plans. What do you say to that, my friend?"

"How very rude," said Prudence, making Abby laugh.

"I couldn't agree more," came a deep voice at Abby's side—a voice that robbed her of her breath and caused her head to spin and her heart to falter. She knew that voice almost as well as her own.

She turned her head slowly in his direction and immediately wished she hadn't. Brigston looked even more handsome than she remembered. His light brown hair fell roguishly across his forehead. His strong jaw, blue-gray eyes, and mischievous smile caused her knees to wobble and quake. How had she not noticed him before now? How had she missed his name being announced or not felt his presence?

She certainly felt it now.

Good grief, she was staring—gaping, more like. At some point her mouth had fallen open, so she snapped it shut and tried to locate her wits. What had he said again?

"Ah, see?" said Prudence, coming to her rescue. "Lord Brigston agrees with me. He, too, thinks you should stop interfering with my meddling."

"I don't think he knows what he agreed to." Somehow, Abby's voice sounded strong and unaffected. Thank goodness.

"What exactly *did* I agree to?" Brigston watched the dancers with an air of nonchalance, as though he were conversing with an acquaintance—one who bored him.

Abby felt a flicker of irritation she couldn't quite keep out of her tone. "That I am behaving badly."

"Are you?"

As soon as his gaze locked on hers, Abby had to remind herself to breathe again. How could he look so calm when she was anything but? His breathing didn't sound erratic, his face wasn't flushed, and he didn't seem to struggle to make conversation while his head threatened to burst.

Life could be vastly unfair at times.

He watched her expectantly, as if waiting for her to say something.

Oh dear, he *was* waiting for her. What had he asked again? Something about her behaving badly? Merciful heavens, why was it so hot in here? Where was a fan when she needed it most?

He was still waiting.

"Er . . ." She stumbled for a response, any response, even a dimwitted one. "I never behave badly."

"Just stubbornly," muttered Prudence, watching her strangely. If Abby didn't pull herself together soon, her friend would be privy to things she didn't wish her to know. Perhaps she already was.

Drat.

Brigston grinned. "I'll attest to that."

Abby frowned. Were they joining forces against *her* now? Honestly, could someone open a door? At the very least, a window?

"Who's made a pact with whom now?" muttered Abby.

"Bless you for coming along when you did, Lord Brigston," said Prudence. "It's about time someone sided with me for a change. Please tell Abby she's not allowed to play the doddering old maid all evening and continue to cry off from dancing."

Brigston leaned near Abby and lowered his voice. "I don't think you look the least bit doddering or old." He made it sound as though he'd just paid her a handsome compliment.

"What a flatterer you are, my lord," she said dryly. "That is high praise indeed."

"Gads, you're right. That was poorly done of me, wasn't it? I suppose I shall have to make it up to you."

"I suppose you will," she said, feeling a little more normal. If only she'd seen him arrive. She could have prepared herself at least a little.

"Would you consider joining me for the next dance if I promise to pepper you with prettier compliments?" he asked.

Prudence quickly added, "If you do, I won't be able to accuse you of behaving like a doddering old maid any longer."

Abby tried to tell herself to refuse him. She tried to remember that he was not hers to have. And she tried to think of all the reasons dancing with him would be a terrible idea. Unfortunately, she really was too compliant.

"I'd love nothing more," she said, then immediately berated herself for being an imbecile.

The minuet came to an end, and the couples on the dance floor began to disperse. Sophia almost made it back to Prudence and Abby when Mr. Rend intercepted her, no doubt to claim her hand for the following set.

The musicians announced the next dance, and Abby's

mouth fell open once again. A waltz? Could that be right? Lady Fernside had always been a stickler for proprieties. She couldn't have possibly condoned a waltz.

Those around Abby appeared equally shocked—all except Brigston, who was grinning like a rogue.

He offered his elbow. "How fortunate. A waltz."

Her eyes narrowed suspiciously. "You don't look surprised."

"Why should I be? The waltz has been gaining popularity for some time now."

"Yes, but this is Lady Fernside's ball, and only last week at Almack's I heard her call the waltz indecent."

"A woman is allowed to change her mind." He pulled her into his solid arms, and Abby forgot to breathe yet again. She was conscious only of his hand on her waist and his lips so close to hers. And oh, that scent of citrus and spice. How she'd missed it.

"If you must know, I came across Lady Fernside in Hyde Park earlier today and heard her complain that the Duke of Honeywell had yet to grace her ballroom with his presence, no pun intended. She seemed distraught by the man's elusiveness, so I came to her aid. We agreed that if I could encourage the duke to attend, she would allow a waltz to be played at her ball. Apparently, she cares more about the duke than her unblemished reputation because she readily agreed."

Brigston intoxicated her. His lively conversation, the way his eyes crinkled when he grinned, the extra line on the left side of his mouth that could be seen only when his lips smiled or spoke certain words. Abby's surroundings became a blur as he spun her around and around.

This is what Heaven must feel like.

"How did you convince the duke to come?" she asked.

"He owed me a favor. I once saved him from making a drunken wager that would have cost him a tidy sum."

Abby knew her mind was befuddled, but . . . "All you asked in return was for him to please Lady Fernside by attending her ball? Goodness, if that is all the repayment you require, I should like to exchange a few favors with you myself."

"Don't be such a nodcock," he said. "The favor had nothing to do with pleasing Lady Fernside and everything to do with pleasing myself. I am now waltzing with you, am I not? And at the home of the most notorious stickler alive, no less. I feel more than compensated."

Abby stared at him. Was he saying he'd orchestrated this waltz so that he might dance it with her?

No, that couldn't possibly be it. But why was he holding her so close and looking at her in that way? Perhaps he'd invented the story to make up for his unflattering compliment before. He did say he'd pepper her with pretty words.

"Abby, are you quite all right? You look pale."

"Just a trifle dizzy is all." After this, she would need to escape to the balcony for several deep breaths of fresh air, not that London air could be described as fresh.

He appeared worried. "Should we sit the rest of the dance out?"

"No," she said a little too quickly and a little too forcefully. Oh dear, she was making a mull of this. Perhaps she should simply be honest with him.

It used to come easier.

"You caught me off guard, Brigston. I wasn't expecting to see you tonight—or waltz with you, for that matter. I'm just a little shaken."

He looked at her with tenderness. "There's the Abby I have missed. It wasn't my intention to unsettle you."

"Well, you did. But at least you have not trod on my slippers as of yet."

"Yet?" He grinned. "Are you expecting me to?"

"If your dancing skills are anything like your shuttle-cock skills . . . well, you did lose to a woman during her confinement, after all."

He laughed. "I might remind you of the tally before you invented a ridiculous rule and declared yourself champion, but that would be ungentlemanly of me."

"Yes, it would," she agreed, and he laughed again. How she'd missed that laugh. How she'd missed him.

"Come riding with me tomorrow," he said, his eyes earnest and pleading.

"Why?" she pressed, wanting him to be as honest with her as she'd been with him.

"I've missed you."

His words thrilled and frightened her at the same time. It felt dangerous, somehow, like standing too close to the edge of a cliff. "I've missed you as well, but . . . would it be wise?"

"What's unwise about an innocent ride through Hyde Park? I have a delightful mare you can borrow, you're no longer with child, and I can't think of a better way for you to tell me what you've been up to these past months. Please say you'll come."

"I suppose when you put it that way . . ." It did sound safer than circling a ballroom in his arms.

"Then it's agreed. I shall collect you at eight tomorrow morning."

She nearly missed a step. "Eight!"

"The park is virtually empty at that hour," he explained. "We can talk without interruption or having to shout."

He made a good point, but it still felt precarious to Abby.

"I don't know," she said. Spending time alone with him would only make it harder to move on with her life. But wasn't this precisely what she'd yearned for? Hadn't she come to London with the hope of seeing him again?

Why did people yearn for things that would only hurt them in the end?

The waltz concluded, but Brigston kept hold of her. "Say you'll ride with me, Abby."

Weak-willed. That's what she was. "I'll ride with you."

He rewarded her with a smile before escorting her back to Prudence. Then he bowed, said his goodbyes, and promptly left the ball. As far as Abby knew, he hadn't danced with anyone else, and judging by the whispers and curious looks cast her way, she wasn't the only one who'd noticed.

An excited Mrs. Gifford rushed up to say, "You'll never guess who's in the card room. The Duke of Honeywell! Can you believe it? He hasn't been to a ball since he married his daughter off over a decade ago, at which point he swore he'd never attend one again. I cannot imagine what prompted him to come tonight. Lady Fernside must be beside herself with glee. What a triumph! People are saying he arrived with Lord Brigston. Do you know anything about it, Abby?"

"I do not, Mrs. Gifford." It was true enough. Abby hadn't known they'd come together or that the duke had come at all. In her mind, it had been an outrageous tale meant only to flatter her.

A strange feeling settled in Abby's stomach, not queasy but not friendly either. She was back on that ledge, looking down and wondering where she'd land if she fell.

Prudence sidled up to her and lowered her voice. "I believe you've been keeping something from me, my friend, and I'm not sure how I feel about it."

Oh no, not this as well. Abby didn't know how much

more she could tolerate. "Please, Pru," she begged, "do not meddle in this."

The obvious distress in her voice seemed to have a sobering effect on her friend. Prudence laid a gentle hand on her arm and softened her voice. "Where there's a will there's a way, you know."

Not always, Abby thought. It had been Prudence's experience that if two people truly loved each other, nothing could keep them apart. That had been the case with her and Knave, as well as the characters in the stories she wrote. But sometimes love came in second to other things, and that was something Prudence didn't understand.

Abby swallowed. "In this, there isn't a way."

That seemed to quiet Prudence, but that was all it did. The music, laughter, voices, and tinkling of crystal that had cheered her earlier now sounded like deafening noise.

TWENTY

HYDE PARK WAS remarkably beautiful for late March in London. The skies were only partially covered in clouds, and a soft breeze stirred the leaves of the oak and cypress trees near Abby. Although she still didn't know what to make of Brigston, her head felt clearer out here in the open. The horse he'd provided her with was a spirited one, and Abby had always loved to ride. It felt like ages since she'd last sat atop a horse.

"Shall we race to that tree yonder?" he asked.

Abby looked to where he pointed at the top of a small rise in the distance. A thrill swept through her at the thought of galloping across the expanse, feeling the wind on her face and the freedom that came from riding fast. It was a sensation one did not usually experience in London.

She fiddled with the pins holding her gray bonnet in place and made sure they were secure.

"If I should win?" she asked.

"That won't happen," he replied. "Swindler has never beat Storm before."

"Swindler? Who decided on such a name? This creature is far too genteel to be called Swindler." She rubbed her gloved hand along the mare's neck.

"You won't say that once you come to know her better," said Brigston. "Now about that race."

"Why should I agree when you've already informed me that my horse cannot outrun your own?"

"Because you're determined to beat me in spite of Swindler's impediments."

"What impediments?" She leaned over to pat her horse once more. "I see nothing wrong with her."

"Good. Then a race it is?"

She studied him suspiciously, noting how splendid he looked in his dark blue coat, buff trousers, and black hessians. She felt a flicker of envy that he no longer had to wear mourning colors while she still had months to go. At least the gray habit she wore didn't make her look as pale.

"Have you taken to cheating to best me, my lord?"

"*If* I've taken to cheating, and I'm not saying I have, I did it only to even the score, lest you forget about our shuttlecock game."

"How could I when you feel the need to mention it every time we meet? One would think you are a sore loser."

"I am," he agreed. "So let's agree to race once and for all, so I can win and feel better about myself." Not many people would describe his speech as charming, but Abby was charmed.

"If you insist," she said. "On the count of three then?"

He gestured for her to continue.

"One . . ." She leaned forward and gripped her whip tightly in her hand. "Two . . ." She snapped the whip against the backside of her horse and smiled when it sprang forward, carrying her across the meadow. If Brigston could openly cheat, so could she.

"Three," she shouted into the wind.

The ground flew past her, and she was halfway across

the clearing before she heard Brigston approach from behind.

"Impediments indeed," she said, urging the animal to quicken its pace. But instead of lurching forward as she expected, the mare began to slow, allowing Storm to break into the lead. By the time Abby arrived at the tree, Swindler had dropped to a pace no faster than a trot. Brigston waited for her, grinning in triumph.

So much for thinking her animal spirited.

"Feel better?" she asked him dryly.

"Much." His horse danced beneath him as though antsy to race again. Abby's mare, on the other hand, was content to munch on some tall grass that had grown through a hedge.

She examined Swindler with a frown. "What did you do, put laudanum in her water? Should I be worried she'll lie down for a nap?"

Brigston laughed. "We purchased her because she had a spirited energy about her. Her name was originally Tempest, you see. But after our groom attempted to exercise her a handful of times, we realized our mistake. She always starts out fast and slows within a minute or two, and no amount of coercion has had any effect on her."

"Hence the name Swindler."

"Now you understand." He was grinning like a fool, and she had the strongest urge to throw something at him. Her whip, perhaps? Followed by her hat and even a boot?

"How kind of you to see me outfitted with a mount who's been properly trained to lose," said Abby.

"I thought you'd be more entertained."

"You overestimated me."

He chuckled and swung down from his horse, signaling to a groom to collect Storm. Then he held out his hand to Abby. "Walk with me?"

He'd asked that exact question months before. Only then they were alone on a long stretch of beach adjacent to the Solent. Now, they were in Hyde Park near the Serpentine. A few others were out and about, but other than that, they were as alone as two people could feel in London.

The moment Brigston took her by the waist to help her down, she knew she would never be able to put her feelings for him aside. Even the most innocent touch stirred a myriad of sensations within her. She tried not to smell, feel, or respond to him, but the aromas of leather, citrus, and spice invaded her senses so much that she lingered with her hands on his shoulders, desperately wanting more.

It was he who finally released her and took a step back, a cold reminder of his place in her life. It wrenched her heart. Why had she agreed to come this morning? Why had she come to London at all? She had yearned to see him again, but now that he stood before her, just out of reach—*always* out of reach—she felt only torment.

He tucked his hands behind his back and began walking at her side. "I can almost imagine we are back at Oakley, strolling along the beach, although the Serpentine smells nothing like the Solent."

"No," said Abby.

"Do you remember the day I caught you riding and insisted you not do so any longer?"

"I remember thinking you a curmudgeon."

"I've always felt sorry about that—not sorry enough to allow you to ride again, obviously—but you were so happy one moment and so annoyed with me the next. I promised myself I would make it up to you someday."

"I see," said Abby. "So this morning's outing was a way for you to assuage a guilty conscience."

"And my pride."

She chuckled and ran her free hand along the top of a recently pruned yew hedge. The needles pricked at her gloves, but she didn't mind. She liked the texture. "You needn't have worried about making it up to me. You were right to stop me from riding. I should not have put Anne in danger like that."

"Tell me about her and your time with Lord and Lady Knave." Brigston sounded genuinely interested, so Abby happily obliged. She told him about her constantly increasing midsection, how she'd misjudge narrow spaces, spill soup or drip preserves down the front of her dresses, and how she'd constantly bump into things. It wasn't a ladylike thing to talk about, but with him it didn't matter. She could talk about anything.

She told him how little Anne had been and how adept she was about expressing her opinions. "I can already tell she's going to be a stubborn thing," said Abby fondly. "I would love for you to meet her at some point. Your mother drops by almost daily now."

"So I've heard." He stopped walking to peer across the Serpentine, and a breeze lifted his hair from his forehead. Abby desperately wanted him to turn to her, take her in his arms, hold her close, and tell her he couldn't live without her. She wished she could tell him the same, but that was one thing she couldn't say.

He released her arm and crouched to pick up a rock that he threw across the Serpentine. It skipped once, twice, three times, before plopping into the wide river.

If there was a skill that Abby had picked up during her unconventional upbringing, it was skipping rocks. She crouched down, sorted through a few rocks before finding a suitable one, and walked to the bank of the river. Taking careful aim, she flung it across the river. It skipped nine times before disappearing into the water. Not her best throw ever, but the rock hadn't been perfectly flat.

She beamed at Brigston, who was staring in astonishment at the place her rock had landed.

"I don't believe we are even any longer, sir," she said.

"You never cease to amaze me, woman. Did the cows teach you that skill?"

"It was the frogs."

He scooped up a handful of rocks and made several more attempts at skipping them, but his longest throw included only seven skips.

He looked back at her with a grimace. "I think you should confess that I'm the real shuttlecock champion."

"Never."

"Wretch."

She giggled. "Do you wish to race the horses again? Would that restore your pride?"

"No, but a shuttlecock rematch might. Would tomorrow be too soon? The ballroom in our townhouse may not be as large as Oakley's, but we could manage a tolerable game."

It was hard to tell if he was in earnest when his eyes glimmered with humor like that. Shuttlecock on a rainy day in the country had been an entertaining diversion, but here in refined and proper London? He had to be jesting.

Either way, she was not at liberty to accept.

"Sophia has asked me to accompany her on a drive with Mr. Rend and Mr. Wallace tomorrow afternoon, and that evening we are attending Mrs. Temple's card party."

He sighed. "It's just as well. I have something that needs doing tomorrow anyway. It's a shame though. I would have preferred shuttlecock."

"Perhaps another time?"

"Perhaps."

During the ride back to Knave's townhouse, the skies seemed to grow gloomier. It felt like a sign of things to come.

TWENTY-ONE

THE FOLLOWING MORNING, Lady Brigston fawned over Anne in the drawing room. Since her first encounter with her grandchild, she'd come most every day Abby was at home, arriving a little before their usual calling hours. Initially, Abby would lead her up to the nursery, but when Lady Brigston continued to come, Abby asked Nurse Lovell to bring Anne down to the more comfortable drawing room. When other callers arrived, they cooed over her daughter as well, at least until Anne began to fuss or howl with displeasure. When that happened, Lady Brigston would clutch her to her chest and quit the room, as though she were Anne's nurse.

Abby had gone after her once in embarrassment, explaining that she'd take Anne back to the nursery, but Lady Brigston had shooed aside her concerns, saying she could return the baby just as easily, then added with a twinkle in her eye, "There are some pleasures grandmothers ought to have, don't you think?"

Abby realized then just how much her mother-in-law was coming to care for Anne. Lady Brigston had always been a stickler. It wasn't like her to exit a room full of visitors without so much as a good day, yet that's precisely what she'd done. When the end of the season came, and Abby secured her own cottage away from Hampshire, how would that affect Lady Brigston?

Abby couldn't help but worry.

"It's effortless to coax a smile from her now," said Lady Brigston as she grinned down at Anne and tickled her chin. A gurgle sounded, and Lady Brigston grinned. "She will laugh soon, I'd wager my hat on it."

The hat in question was a deep violet with large ostrich plumes jutting up from one side and towering overtop, the way a palm frond would do. It wasn't Abby's style, but the matching violet gown with a gold ribbing was quite pretty.

"You have an irresistible smile, my darling girl," Lady Brigston said to Anne. "You must use that to your advantage. No matter how naughty you might behave, only smile, and no one will be able to stay cross with you for long."

"I'm not sure I care for that advice, Lady Brigston," said Abby.

"Care for it or not, it's a grandmother's prerogative to indulge one's grandchild. I do wish you'd call me Mother. At the very least, Anne, though that could cause some confusion."

Abby stared at her mother-in-law in surprise. The request had been spoken in such a casual manner, the way one might mention a bit of gossip or unremarkable news. *I should like to invite the Markhams to dine. Do you approve?*

For Abby, however, it had been more than remarkable. It had been overwhelming and humbling.

Mother. Abby tried the word out in her mind and found she liked the sound of it. It felt a little foreign, but in time, that would surely lessen.

"I would love that above all things . . . Mother."

Lady Brigston continued to tickle Anne's chin, but her

smile widened, as though she liked the sound of it as well. It was a sweet moment that Abby would always cherish. Mother, daughter, granddaughter.

This is only the beginning, she thought.

The clock chimed the hour, and Abby glanced at it in surprise. Where on earth was Prudence? Callers would arrive soon, and they'd be vastly disappointed if the lady of the house did not attend to them.

As if on cue, Prudence burst into the room, excitedly waving a letter of some sort. "Only look what Knave just received in this morning's post! It's from Goyle and Parson. They're interested in publishing *Missives and Mayhem* on commission!" She thrust the letter at Abby, her body trembling with excitement. "Can you imagine? I'm beside myself with anticipation. Only think how wonderful it will be to see my name printed on a book!"

Abby took the letter and skimmed its contents. "What does it mean to publish on commission?"

"That I, or rather, Knave, will pay to have it published, and Goyle and Parson will receive ten percent of the commissions. The rest will come to us."

Abby glanced nervously at her mother-in-law—no, it was *mother* now—who was blinking at Prudence in astonishment. "You're having a book published?"

"A romance, to be precise. Isn't it exciting?"

Lady Brigston looked anything but excited, and Abby felt a little abashed. She hadn't told her mother about Prudence's love for the written word or her desire to have stories published. The ton frowned upon trade in any form, be it selling wares on the street or a book in a store. Lady Brigston frowned upon it as well, judging by the look of appall on her face. Abby could almost hear the woman's thoughts.

The wife of an earl publishing a book to be sold? Scandalous.

"I've been writing for ages," said Prudence, "but I never expected to see my stories in print. Now, thanks to the workings of my dear husband, it may actually come to pass. I can scarce believe it!"

Abby was thrilled for her friend. She only wished Prudence had waited until after Lady Brigston had left to announce her good news. Her mother had turned a worrisome shade of green, as though the thought of an acquaintance entering trade made her ill. Abby was hard-pressed not to smile. She, too, had been surprised by her friend's wish to be published, but if anyone could tolerate public censure with aplomb, it was Prudence.

"Will you use a name other than your own?" asked Abby, hoping to appease her mother a little. "You could be like that writer of *Sense and Sensibility.*"

"Why would I do such a thing when it vexes me greatly?" asked Prudence. "I would love nothing more than to write the woman and tell her how much I adore her work—*Pride and Prejudice* was even more diverting than her first—but how can I when she hides behind such an ambiguous name as *A Lady*? Oh, how I wish she wouldn't. I would invite her to tea and beg her to discuss books with me."

"Oh my." Lady Brigston looked faint.

Abby tensed, ready to rescue Anne should the woman succumb to a fit of the vapors. "Would you like me to ring for Nurse Lovell, Mother?" she offered. "Anne did not sleep well last night and will probably grow weary soon."

That seemed to bring Lady Brigston back to her senses. She gathered the baby closer for inspection. "She doesn't appear drowsy to me. I shall tend to her a while longer, I think."

By the time she looked back at Prudence, her color was restored. "Are you not concerned with your reputation, Lady Knave?"

Prudence waved a hand in a careless fashion. "A person's life would be dull indeed without a little scandal attached to her name."

"This will be more than a little," said Lady Brigston. "There will be ramifications. You may be shunned by all of society."

"Not all, I think," Prudence said with a smile. "My husband will still think well of me, along with his parents and my own. Sophia will still be my sister and Abby my dearest friend." She looked pointedly at Abby. "Or are you planning to cut me off when my name appears on a book?"

"Only if you do not cease your matchmaking attempts," said Abby good-naturedly.

"Ah, see?" Prudence grinned at Lady Brigston. "Abby *is* a dear friend. There are also others who will stand by me as well. As to the rest, I don't care a groat for their good opinion. The respect of my husband, family, and close friends is all I require."

If Abby thought her mother would argue this point, she was mistaken. Lady Brigston lapsed into a contemplative silence. After a moment or two she looked down at Anne and murmured, "How nice it would be to care only about the opinions of those who care about you."

THE SMELL OF smoke, drink, and something foul met Morgan as he stepped into the tavern with the Bow Street Runner he'd hired months ago, a Mr. Dyer. The man was rugged and rough-looking, with a crooked nose, several days'

worth of growth around his mouth, and a jagged scar above his left eye—not that any of that mattered to Morgan. The man had done his job well and with discretion.

During the past several months, Dyer had tracked down a scoundrel by the name of William Penroth in a village called Danset, two hours south of London. He'd also located another woman willing to testify against him. Apparently she'd suffered a similar fate as Abby and longed to see the man brought to justice.

"There." Dyer pointed a gnarled finger towards a table on the other side of the room, where three men sat playing cards. The youngest had to be Penroth. He was about Abby's age and had a depraved look about him. His coat lay in a heap on the filthy floor, and his cravat hung loose and wrinkled about his neck, as though he'd been there a while. His hair was disheveled, and his black eyes had the look of a drunkard. Morgan's hands clenched into fists as he thought of what the blackguard had done to Abby. How satisfying it would be to pummel him within an inch of his life.

Dyer had said he could manage the arrest on his own, but Morgan had insisted on accompanying the man. He wanted to see the look on Penroth's face when he realized his freedom was about to be snatched away.

A bar maid sashayed past the table, wearing a dirty, low-cut dress. Penroth tucked his cards under his leg, grabbed her hand, and pulled her onto his lap. "Where do you think you're going?" he drawled, leering at her.

She smiled and tugged on his cravat, pulling his mouth to hers. He returned the kiss greedily, his hands roaming wherever they wished.

A grizzly man to the left rolled his eyes and growled, "Your turn, Penroth."

Penroth broke free, grabbed his cards, and tried to see

around the woman on his lap, but when she attempted to kiss him again, he grumbled, "Out of my way," and shoved her to the floor. She landed in a disgruntled heap while he went back to examining his cards as though nothing had happened.

Morgan seethed inwardly. He walked to the bar maid and offered a hand to help her to her feet. She glared at Penroth before turning a seductive smile on Morgan. When she began twining her fingers through his hair, he took her by the hands and nodded in the direction of the kitchen. "Go," he said, in a kind but stern voice.

She pouted and pushed past him, moving in the opposite direction, no doubt anxious to find another man who'd be interested in her charms. It was how she made her livelihood, but Morgan wondered if she ever wished for a different, better life. Did she even know the possibility existed? Probably not.

'Twas a shame.

Penroth glared at Morgan and Dyer with wary, bloodshot eyes. "What do you want?" he snarled at Dyer. No doubt he'd spied the pair of manacles dangling at Dyer's side.

"Are you William Penroth?" Dyer asked, even though he already knew the answer.

Penroth laid down his cards and leaned back in his chair. "Who wants to know?"

"That's of no importance to you," Dyer said.

"It's also of no importance to me that I tell you my name," he drawled, examining his cards once more.

"He's Penroth," confirmed the grizzly man at his side, adding, "I want no trouble."

"I'm only here for him," said Dyer, grabbing Penroth by the collar and hauling him to his feet.

"What's the meaning of this? Unhand me!" Penroth

jerked one hand free and threw an awkward punch at Dyer, who dodged it deftly and grabbed him again, this time with a stronger grip. Manacles were slapped on his wrists, and Dyer jerked him close. "Happy to oblige if the magistrate rules it so, but something tells me you won't be so lucky."

It was a shame Penroth appeared too drunk to remember much of this tomorrow. Morgan would love this moment to be branded in his mind forever.

The pig.

Ah, there it was. Hatred. Scorn. Fear. Good. He wasn't too drunk to feel.

As Dyer dragged him from the tavern, Penroth's attempts to resist became frenzied. He knocked over several chairs and a table, spilling ale from a tankard across the uneven floor. But he was no match for Dyer, who was both sober and stronger. In a matter of seconds, Penroth was tossed unceremoniously into a rented carriage.

Dyer slammed the door and locked it from the outside before looking back at Morgan. "Will there be anything else, my lord?" He didn't sound even a little out of breath.

Good man. Morgan had picked the right runner for this job. He held out his hand. "Many thanks, Dyer. You will be well compensated for your trouble."

Dyer accepted his hand and gave it a solid shake. "Always happy to put away a scoundrel."

"Just be sure you keep him locked up for a good long while."

"Shouldn't be a problem. The local magistrate has no tolerance for crimes against innocent women, especially a lady."

"Glad to hear it. I shall meet you back here on Friday next."

Dyer grunted, then climbed onto the driver's seat and

spurred the horses forward. Morgan waited until the carriage was out of sight before he walked down the road to the inn, where his groom waited with the horses.

He was now one step closer.

TWENTY-TWO

HIS MOTHER'S VOICE came from the darkened drawing room. "Morgan, is that you?"

He squinted to see her, but the room was black. No candles were lit and no fire smoldered in the grate.

He lit a lamp on the side table and carried it into the room, finally spying her in a chair near the fireplace. She wore a dressing gown, cap, and slippers, and had a quilt draped over her lap.

"What are you doing up at this hour?" he asked. It was half past four in the morning. Had something happened?

"I was waiting for you," she said calmly, gesturing to the chair at her side. "Sit, Morgan, there are things we need to discuss."

Morgan knew if he sat down, he'd be hard pressed to get up again. He blinked weary eyes at his parent. "Can this not wait until morning? Or better still, afternoon?"

"I value my sleep as much as you do and will not sleep a wink until I have unburdened myself. Sit."

Morgan sighed, placed the candle on the mantle, and collapsed on the chair next to his mother. He leaned forward and rested his head against his palms, waiting for her to speak.

"I learned today that you made an appearance at Lady Fernside's ball."

Morgan groaned inwardly. He had known word would reach his mother eventually. He just didn't plan on being confronted about it at four o'clock in the morning.

"I did," he said.

"Did you also ignore most everyone, solicit Abby's hand for the waltz—which Lady Fernside swears you requested—and leave immediately after?"

Morgan frowned. From her accounting, his behavior sounded like that of a madman. In truth, he *had* felt reckless that evening, but certainly not mad. On the contrary, he'd never felt more sane in his life.

"I spoke to several people, and I didn't leave immediately following the dance," he countered. "I paused to pay my respects to Lady Fernside on my way out." Perhaps "several people" had been a slight exaggeration. In reality, he'd exchanged some half-hearted pleasantries with those who'd waylaid him, then moved on quickly. He'd been more focused on locating Abby than making conversation. But his mother needn't know that.

"Did it not occur to you that your actions were tantamount to making Abby an offer? Only you can't offer for her, can you, because it is against the law!" She rubbed her temples with her fingers and grimaced. "You set the tongues to wagging across all of London, and did you think to prepare me for the onslaught? No. Earlier today, I sat here in complete shock with no idea how to explain your motives."

Morgan felt a pang of guilt. He supposed he should have prepared her, but if anyone could handle an onslaught, as she put it, it was his mother. He was certain she'd managed to disguise her shock and come up with some sort of explanation for her son's erratic behavior.

"I'm sorry, Mother. If you are worried about my reputation—"

"I'm not as concerned with your reputation as I am with Abby's. You are a marquess and will weather scandal in time, but Abby will be made to bear the scars for some time. People are speculating that you have taken her as your mistress. I despise speaking plainly about such matters, but you've given me no choice. A widow's reputation may not be as delicate as an innocent's, but Abby is my daughter, and I will not have her suffer by your hand. Honestly, Morgan, I have never been more appalled by your behavior in my life."

Morgan ought to feel more repentant, but he hadn't walked into Lady Fernside's ball in a state of naivety. Rather, the entire evening had been a calculated move on his part to *cause* talk. He wanted the ton to know of his interest in Abby. Let them believe the worst in her for now. In time, all would be set to rights—or at least he'd planned for that outcome.

"I intend to marry her, Mother."

His announcement was met with silence. Resignation crossed her features, as though she'd been expecting him to say as much while hoping he would not.

"What about your inheritance?" she asked.

"I have learned that if we marry overseas—perhaps Paris—our marriage will be binding and uncontestable. The laws are different there, and—"

"Paris?" she asked faintly. Morgan knew what she was thinking. Another elopement. More talk. More conjecture. How much could their family bear?

With any luck, a little more.

The ton thrived on scandal but didn't like being ambushed by it. It made them feel obtuse when they preferred to be thought of as clever. At Lady Fernside's ball,

Morgan had made his interest in Abby known—something he would continue to do over the next several weeks. The ton would draw whatever conclusions they wished, but when at last he and Abby returned from Paris as man and wife, society would not feel duped. Rather, he fully expected many to claim they'd deduced his intentions and weren't at all surprised.

With any luck, Abby would become the notorious wife of the Marquess of Brigston instead of an ostracized woman.

"I know this is not the direction you'd have chosen for my life, but I could never marry another. I love her."

His mother looked down at her lap, and a ringlet fell forward, shrouding one eye. The other appeared troubled. Morgan felt a pang of sympathy for her. All her life, she'd maintained a reputation that was above reproach, and she'd expected the same from her children. Unfortunately, both her sons had disappointed her in that respect.

Morgan leaned forward and took hold of her hand. "Say you'll support me in this," he whispered. "I need you."

She looked up at him and actually smiled a little. "How is it that one woman can be the cause of so much mischief in our family? If I did not care for Abby as much as I do, I'd despise her. But if truth be known, I might even like her better than you."

Morgan chuckled. "I'm not surprised."

She sobered quickly, drawing in a shuddering breath. "It's hard for me not to care about my standing with the ton—I've been raised to value it above all else—but if marriage to Abby will make you both happy, I will support you. I will also look forward to having little Anne at Oakley with us. I feared I would have to let her go at the season's end, and I have dreaded that day from the first moment I held her in my arms."

Morgan couldn't say he understood because he'd never seen the child. "Does she look like her mother?"

"The bluest eyes you've ever seen, and the tiniest golden curls. She's an angel, even when she howls something terrible."

Morgan smiled, but there was a reason he hadn't yet called on Abby or asked to see Anne. If the child took after her father at all, Morgan wasn't sure he could ever look upon her without the loathing he carried for William Penroth.

"Is it difficult to love her, knowing how her existence came about?" Morgan asked, voicing one of his greatest fears.

His mother did not hesitate. "Oddly enough, it has made her easier to love. She is like the first flower that blooms in the spring, so vibrant and beautiful. She is the light in the darkness, the good in the bad. How can that be hard to love?"

Morgan was touched by her words. Abby had said something similar to him long ago, and while he'd admired her sentiments at the time, he couldn't fathom she'd truly feel that way when the child came.

He'd been wrong.

"You should call on Abby and ask to see her," said his mother. "I'll wager my favorite bonnet you will be charmed in an instant."

"What the deuce would I do with your favorite bonnet?" Morgan asked dryly.

His mother peered at him in confusion, then burst out laughing. She covered her mouth with her hands, but when that didn't stifle her laughter, she doubled over, smothering it in the quilt on her lap. When at last she lifted her head, tears of joy leaked from the corners of her eyes.

"Forgive me," she gasped. "I just pictured you wearing a bonnet and—" She burst into giggles once more.

Morgan smiled, mustered the energy to move, and drew himself up. He held a hand out to his mother. "I will do as you suggest in time. For now, I think we should take ourselves off to bed, or you are likely to suffer an apoplexy from too much amusement."

She tucked her arm through his and allowed him to lead her from the room, but when they reached the staircase, she stopped him. "I suddenly feel famished and can't stop thinking about the chocolate cake Cook served for dessert. I am going to indulge in another slice before bed."

The mention of cake made Morgan hesitate as well. He glanced up the stairs, weighing his options, before grinning at his mother. "I believe I will join you."

TWENTY-THREE

ABBY PLACED ANNE in Brigston's arms and nervously watched his face, searching for any signs of discomfort. It had only been a few days since their morning ride through the park, but he had finally called and asked to see the baby. She'd excitedly led him up to the nursery, but now that he awkwardly cradled her little girl, she realized just how much she wanted him to love Anne.

He looked so masculine in his dark tailored coat and pristine white shirt, but with her baby in his arms, he appeared fatherly as well. The sight might have melted her heart if he didn't also appear so anxious.

Goodness, what was the matter with him? One would think he'd never held an infant before. Hmm . . . perhaps he hadn't.

"She takes after her mother," he said, his voice unnaturally bright.

Abby looked at him strangely, wishing he would say what was truly on his mind. "She has my disposition as well—sweet unless provoked."

He chuckled and shifted Anne from one arm to the other, looking ill at ease. Abby could only imagine what he might be thinking, all of which caused her to snicker.

He frowned at her. "What do you find so amusing?"

"You, or rather your expressions," she said. "It's as though you've been given a foreign object and have no idea what to do with it."

He smiled a little. "She's peering up at me as though she knows something I do not. It's disconcerting."

Abby laughed. "She would never presume to know more than a marquess."

He examined Anne once more. "Something tells me she presumes a great deal. I should be grateful she hasn't learned how to speak."

As if in protest, Anne began to fuss and squirm. Brigston was quick to pass her to Nurse Lovell, who sat in the rocking chair not far from them. The nurse coddled and cooed, and Anne soon quieted.

Abby tried not to feel too disheartened. After all, she couldn't expect everyone to take to Anne the way her mother had done, but Brigston's opinion mattered more to her than anyone else's, and she wanted him to adore her baby as much as she did.

Give it time, she told herself firmly.

As they exited the nursery, Brigston stopped her in the hall with a hand on her arm. "Is there somewhere we can speak privately?" His gaze bounced from left to right as though he was nervous about something.

Her arm burned where his hand rested, but despite her best efforts to stamp it down, hope flared. She could only think of one reason he would asked to speak privately, and the thought sent a flurry of butterflies through her stomach.

You're wrong, she told herself. *Nothing has changed.* The Marriage Act had not been repealed, Anne had not been born a boy, and Brigston's cousin was still at liberty to contest a marriage between them. Abby had absolutely no reason to hope for anything in that quarter, but how could she not? He'd danced the waltz with her, taken her riding, asked to see Anne, and now wanted a tête-à-tête. What did it mean?

Abby led him into the breakfast parlor, which had been cleared of people and food hours before. She waited nervously, clenching her fingers. *Say you love me and cannot live without me. Say you want to marry me in spite of that fool law. Say you've found a way to make it happen.*

"We need to talk about William Penroth."

Abby felt the blood drain from her face. William? She hadn't heard or spoken that name in months and had no desire to speak it now. Why would Brigston feel the need to discuss him?

"What about him?" Her voice was cold and not the least bit pleased.

He pulled a chair out and gestured for her to take a seat. When she declined, he pushed it back into place and rested his elbows on the back of it.

"Last September, I secured the services of a Bow Street Runner, one Mr. Dyer. At my bequest, he's been investigating Penroth for months now and has finally built a case that has brought about his arrest. Dyer has discovered two other women who have suffered similarly to you, but only one is willing to tell her story to the magistrate. She's a farmer's daughter, a tenant of Penroth's current employer."

Abby felt bushwhacked. Brigston had secured a Runner? Why hadn't he told her? Why was he explaining all this to her now? Did he think she'd wish to know? Because she didn't. She never wanted to hear that man's name again.

"Abby, a statement from a farmer's daughter will probably not be enough to convict him. Mr. Dyer is hoping that you will be willing to share your experience with the magistrate as well. You can write it all down in a letter, or I can take you to him. It's your choice."

She stared at him even as her heart puddled at her feet. *This* was what he'd needed to talk to her privately about? Where was his confession of love, his solution to their impossible situation?

She closed her eyes and gulped in air, her ire rising with each and every breath. How could he ask this of her? Did he truly expect her to face William again or recount the details of that dreadful night to some unknown magistrate? What of Anne? Would it come to light that William had fathered a child?

The thought sickened her. She would rather walk across hot coals then make him privy to that knowledge.

Abby looked at the man who had held her trust so completely only minutes before. Why had he not spoken of this before now? Why had she not heard of this Mr. Dyer? Why had he not asked for her opinion on the matter? She had trusted him with her story, only to discover that he had passed it along to at least one other without her consent. How *could* he?

Light fell across the corner of the gleaming, wooden table, highlighting a smudge. There had been a time when she'd felt like that spot—unclean and blemished. She used to wake up in a cold panic, with William's face at the forefront of her mind, but it had been a long while since that had happened. She'd thought that was a good sign, that she'd finally put it behind her, but the mere mention of his name brought those horrible feelings back again.

Once again, Abby felt like that smudge. She shuddered at the thought of William, what he'd done to her, what he could still do to her—what he could do to Anne.

She set her jaw and lifted her chin. "The other woman's explanation will have to be enough. I will not face him again,

I will not speak of him, and I would die before I make him aware of Anne's existence. Good day to you, sir."

"Abby, you don't need to see him, and he need never know about—"

Abby was through listening. She brushed past him and strode from the room. He called after her, but she ignored him and quickened into a run, racing to her bedchamber as though the devil was after her. Only after she had closed and bolted the door did she drop to the floor, tuck her knees to her chest, and let the tears come.

ABBY LAY ON her bed, curled into a ball, when the door opened and Prudence and Sophia entered. Prudence flopped down on her stomach next to Abby and propped her chin up with her palms while Sophia took up a more ladylike position at the foot of the bed.

Prudence studied Abby for a moment before speaking. "An hour ago, Lord Brigston quit the house like a man spurned, and now we find you here, looking so puffy and swollen. What has occurred? Did he make you an offer? Never say you have refused him or I shall beat you with a fire poker."

Abby closed her eyes. The last thing she wanted to do was relive that horrible scene, but if there was one thing she knew, her friends would not rest until she confided in them.

Doing her best to keep the emotion from her voice, she said, "Brigston has hired a Runner and found two other women William took advantage of as well. He wants me to speak to a magistrate."

Sophia's eyes widened, while Prudence lifted her head in surprise—pleased surprise, from the looks of it. "He did all that on your behalf? Mercy, he really does care for you."

For a moment, Abby had no words, then her anger came spilling out like a downpour. "He did all of that without my knowledge, Pru, without my consent. Not only did he break a confidence, but he ambushed me with the news, when I was so sure that . . ." She closed her eyes to fight the fresh onslaught of tears. "It took months for the nightmares to subside, several months more for the anger to go with it. But now it has all come back, plaguing me as it did in the past. How can you possibly say those are the actions of a caring man?"

That was the hardest part for Abby. He'd danced and romanced and flattered her, letting her believe one thing, then dropped her on her head the next.

"Because they *are* the actions of a caring man," Prudence insisted.

Sophia's response was more sympathetic. "I'm sure he didn't want to elevate your hopes should nothing come of the investigation."

"Do not speak to me of hope," said Abby. "It has let me down more times than I can count."

Prudence may have rolled her eyes. Abby couldn't quite tell. "I'm certain you haven't had your hopes dashed that many times," she said wryly.

"Pru," her sister chided.

Prudence had the grace to look abashed. "Forgive me, Abby. I simply see things differently. Perhaps Lord Brigston should have asked for your consent, but would you have given it? Even if you had, what if, as Sophia said, nothing came of the investigation? You would have been made to worry and wonder all this time—something Lord Brigston saved you from doing. He even hired a Runner. Do you honestly believe he did that for himself? William Penroth did not violate Lord Brigston. He violated *you* in the most despicable way possible and should be made to pay for his crimes. I can only applaud Lord Brigston for making sure that he does."

"You mentioned he has injured at least two others," added Sophia gently. "Would you wish your fate upon even more women?"

Abby scooted to the head of her bed and pulled her knees to her chest. Of course she didn't want that. "I just want him out of my life."

"Then speak to the magistrate," said Sophia. "Tell him what William did to you, and see to it that he can never harm you or another woman again."

"We will go with you," added Prudence. "We will stand at your side, hold your hand if we must, and see you through this. Do not let him go free, Abby."

In her heart, Abby knew they were right. Speaking out would be the only way to ensure William never hurt another, and hadn't Brigston said she wouldn't have to face him again? Abby had been so angry, she hadn't paid him much heed. If only he'd been upfront with her in the beginning.

She finally nodded. "I will go."

Prudence grinned and rolled off the bed. "I will send word to Brigston that we will be ready as soon as possible."

Abby opened her mouth to waylay her friend, but Prudence was already out the door. Abby turned to Sophia instead. "As soon as possible?" For all Abby knew, that could mean tomorrow, and would she truly be ready by then? Would she ever be ready?

Sophia clasped her hand. "The sooner we go, the sooner you can be done with this thing."

The wise words echoed through Abby's mind. All these months she thought she *had* been done with William Penroth, but she hadn't, not really. She could see that now.

Every now and again, a worry would nip at her heels. Would he appear out of the blue at some social function? Would he discover Anne was his child? Would he try to take her away? Would he do the same to another woman?

Abby already knew the answer to that one. It sickened her.

If only *she'd* been the one to go to a Runner in the weeks following the incident. If she had, could she have prevented the suffering of those other women?

She didn't know. What she did know was that there was something she could do about it now.

TWENTY-FOUR

THREE DAYS LATER, Abby found herself en route to Danset. She'd been told the journey would take over two hours, but it seemed as though she only just climbed into the carriage when it stopped at their destination. Brigston opened the door, holding out his hand to help her down. He and Knave had ridden alongside the carriage while the ladies kept each other company.

Abby hesitated taking his hand. Other than a quick good morning, she hadn't spoken to him since the day he'd broken the news to her. She wasn't sure if she'd forgiven him, but the sight of him still made her heart skip and her breath catch. It was vastly annoying.

"Thank you for coming, Abby," he said. "The magistrate is waiting for us inside."

Her stomach tossed and turned, reminding her of the early days of her confinement when mild bouts of sickness would strike her at random intervals.

"Only a few more steps to go," prodded Prudence, who was seated at her side. Sophia offered an encouraging smile as well.

Abby inhaled deeply and took Brigston's hand, drawing strength from all those who'd come to support her as she descended the steps. Danset was a quaint village surrounded by rolling hills and dense pockets of wilderness. There was a strange smell in the air, a mixture of florals and unique spices. Separately, the scents would have been pleasant, but together they wrinkled Abby's nose.

Brigston nodded at the adjacent building. "That shop sells very strong perfumes."

"Let us hope it wafts into the room where William is being held. He never cared for perfumes."

Brigston smiled. "Shall I purchase several of the more toxic scents and asked that they be left outside his cell?"

"I would like that."

"I might purchase a bottle as well," added Sophia. "It might come in handy when I do not wish to dance with certain men."

"And risk repelling the charming ones as well?" asked her sister. "I will not let you."

Abby was grateful for the banter. It helped to settle her nerves, but she was also anxious to get on with it. Brigston must have sensed her anxiety because he ushered everyone inside.

The first room they entered was dark, dank, and had a dreary quality about it. The windows were too small for a grown person to fit through, and several cracks ran up the stone walls. A young woman sat on a chair in the far shadows, but Abby didn't give her more than a second glance. She was too focused on following Brigston down a narrow hallway. Near the end, he rapped on a closed, wooden door.

A man in dark, nondescript clothes opened it. He had the look of a person who'd seen the worst in mankind yet still believed in the good. Mr. Dyer, Abby assumed before Brigston formally introduced them. The group was directed into a room, where a magistrate sat behind a large oak desk.

He looked like his desk—old and worn, with lines etched into his face and imperfections scattered about. The white powdered wig he wore sat askew, not quite covering the edges of his gray-streaked hair beneath.

He squinted at the group through gold-rimmed spectacles. "Which of you is . . ." He glanced down at his paper. "Lady Jasper?"

Abby stepped forward. "I am." Sophia and Prudence stepped up as well, one on either side, while Brigston and Knave remained behind. Abby appreciated the gesture, though now that she was finally here, she felt perfectly fine. She was ready to tell her story.

The magistrate made sure the three women were comfortably situated on chairs before the questions began. *When did you first meet William Penroth? What was your opinion of him at that time? Did he strike you as dangerous in any way?*

Looking back, Abby could see so clearly now. His outbursts of temper, his jealousy of other men, his desire to control her. She hadn't noticed any of those things at the time. She'd merely seen an attractive man who'd made her life less lonely.

The magistrate continued questioning her, slowly piecing together her interactions with William. He listened, scribbled, and nodded, and Abby found it surprisingly easy to explain the events leading up to her elopement with Jasper. She wouldn't describe the magistrate as sympathetic, but he wasn't brusque either. He was honest.

When she finally told him all she knew, he peered across his desk at her.

"Do you have any sort of proof of your accusations? Did you happen to keep the letters Penroth sent you?"

Abby reached inside her reticule and pulled out a

handful of notes tied with a string. On first glance, they probably looked like cherished letters from a loved one, but if one were to examine them closely, they'd see only crisp pages. Abby had read each missive once before shoving them into an old hat box, never to be looked at again.

"I saved every one," she said. "I'm not sure why. I wanted to toss them into the fire, but something kept me from doing that. Intuition, perhaps?"

The magistrate took them from her, saying in a kind voice, "You were wise to keep them. I thank you for coming all this way to explain in person, Lady Jasper. I will be in touch through Dyer should I require anything more from you."

Abby nodded, feeling a heavy weight lift from her shoulders. As she followed the others from the office, she got a better look at the girl in the corner. Beleaguered straw bonnet, dirty and torn dress, large dark eyes, and an even larger belly.

As soon as the woman caught Abby's eye, she sprang to her feet and approached. "Are you Lady Jasper?"

"Yes," said Abby, recognizing the same wearied and haunted look she'd seen in her own eyes many times before. "You must be Theodosia."

"Aye, milady. Theodosia Green, but most call me Theo. I spoke with the magistrate this mornin' but asked Mr. Dyer if I could wait 'ere for you." Her lips trembled and tears sparkled in her eyes. "I wanted to thank you, milady. For comin'. After Will was finished with me, he turned his sights on my sister. She's only fourteen, but prettier than me, and I knew 'twas only a matter of time before—" She covered her mouth with her hand to stifle a sob. Then she quickly curtsied again. "Thank you ever so much, milady."

She started to walk away, but something within Abby cried out to her.

"Theo," she asked, stopping the girl. "How old are you?"

"Seventeen."

"Do you . . . I mean, are you well cared for?"

Theo's tear-filled eyes looked everywhere but at Abby. "I'm well enough. My pa wanted nothin' to do with me after he'd seen I was increasin', but a neighbor took pity on me. 'E's lettin' me sleep in 'is barn."

"A barn!" Prudence exclaimed in a horrified voice, causing Theo to duck her head in shame.

Knave took his wife by the arm. "We will wait for you outside, Abby." Sophia left as well, her expression more sorrowful than horrified. Brigston, on the other hand, remained at Abby's side, placing a comforting hand against her back.

"Do you really sleep in a barn?" Abby asked.

Theo's bonnet shook when she nodded, looking as though it would fall to pieces any moment. "There's no room for me in the house, but the barn's not so bad. The 'ay keeps me warm enough, and cows are good listeners."

Abby smiled even as her heart constricted. Judging by the size of the girl's belly, it wouldn't be long until her child was born. "How soon until your lying in?"

Theo shrugged. "I've got no way of knowin'. It's gettin' harder and harder to breathe, though, so that must mean soon."

"I remember thinking the same thing," said Abby.

Theo smiled a little, then glanced at the door. "I best be goin'. It's time to milk the cows."

"You have a job then?" Brigston asked.

She nodded. "I milk and tend to the animals in exchange for food and a place to sleep."

"What will you do when the child comes?" he asked.

Theo looked away. "Give it to another, same as Natty did."

Abby had no idea who Natty was or why she'd had to give up her child. But she knew that standing before her was a girl who had been dealt a wicked blow and had been made to suffer even more as a result. Theo hadn't received an offer of marriage. She hadn't been blessed with friends like Prudence or Sophia. From the sounds of it, she didn't even have a mother.

What would become of her if Abby walked out that door? She didn't want to think about it.

"Tell me, Theo," said Abby. "What sort of work did you do before?"

"I looked after my siblings, did the washin' and mendin', cooked, and cleaned. Ma died a few years back, and I was doin' her work 'til Pa sent me away."

"Now all that work has fallen to your sister?" Brigston guessed.

She nodded. "Wish I could do somethin' to 'elp, but Pa won't 'ear of it. Suzie comes to visit me when she can. She even brought an old quilt for when the babe comes."

Suzie must be Theo's younger sister. Abby was slowly piecing together the tragedy that had become this girl's life— all because of one selfish, dishonorable man. Abby hoped he'd rot in prison for a good, long while.

"Theo, I've been looking for a woman with your skills," said Abby. "I will be acquiring a cottage of my own soon, and I'll be in need of a maid of all work. I think you'd suit perfectly."

Theo looked down at her round belly then back to Abby, staring at her as though she'd gone daft.

Abby smiled. "You wouldn't be expected to start until after your lying in, of course. In the meantime, I will put you up at the inn and see that you are looked after by the local doctor. Once the child arrives, we will find it a good home.

We can even try to find one near the cottage, if you'd like to be nearby."

Theo's eyes grew wide. "Do you mean it, milady?"

"I do."

Tears sparkled in Theo's eyes, along with something else—hope, the sort of hope that wouldn't fall prey to disappointment. Abby would see to that.

Theo wiped at her eyes. "I 'eard the parson and 'is wife 'ave been wantin' a child somethin' desperate. The entire parish's been prayin' for them, sayin' they're deservin' of good fortune. Do you think they'd want the child?"

Abby thought of Anne, how difficult it would have been to give her up, and how lucky she'd been not to have to make that choice. Theo, on the other hand, was not as lucky, but instead of feeling sorry for herself, she wanted to give her child a better life.

If Abby had any doubts about helping this girl, they diminished in an instant. "I'm sure they'll treasure your child as their own."

Theo's shoulders straightened a little, as though a burden had been lifted. Abby knew that look well. She reached out and touched Theo's shoulder. "Come. Let's get you settled at the inn and summon that doctor. We can also send word to your sister and neighbor about your change in circumstances."

"I . . . I don't know what to say," Theo said.

"You don't have to say anything."

"Oh, but I do. Thank you ever so much, milady."

Abby extended the thanks to Brigston with a smile, her heart warm and full. If it wasn't for his interference and generosity with her annuity, William Penroth would still be free and Theo would be made to deliver her baby among the cows. If she wasn't sure she'd forgiven him before, she was now.

TWENTY-FIVE

SOMETHING ODD IS afoot, thought Abby when Sophia and Prudence exchanged another secretive smile. The three women were in Prudence's carriage, jostling through a London street with rain pouring overhead and streaking down the panes of the small windows. Abby felt bad for the coachman, whose only protection was a hat and heavy coat, but Sophia and Prudence had insisted on a drive to combat the dreariness of the day, or so they said. They both appeared too happy for Abby to truly believe it.

The carriage jolted to a stop, and Prudence pressed her nose to the window excitedly. "Here we are," she announced.

Abby looked through the rain-splattered window to see an unfamiliar townhouse. "I wasn't aware we had a destination."

"We always have a destination," said Prudence.

"You made no mention of that before. You only said it was too dreary to stay at home and we should take a drive instead."

"And so we have."

Abby rolled her eyes and looked to Sophia for help instead. "Would you be kind enough to enlighten me, Soph? I don't believe I have ever been to this house before."

231

Sophia opened her mouth to say something, but her sister cut her off. "That is for us to know and you to find out."

Sophia only shrugged and smiled.

The coachman pulled open the door, and rain rushed in, splattering Abby's skirts and the floor of the coach. He carried an umbrella but didn't appear nearly as cheerful as Prudence.

"I'll take you up first, Lady Jasper," he said, holding a hand out to Abby.

Bless your soul, Abby thought as she climbed from the carriage and hurried up the steps. A tall and lanky man she assumed was the butler held the door open and ushered her quickly inside. She was shaking some of the rain from her skirts when the door closed behind her. She turned to find the butler standing like a guard in front of it.

"I can collect your coat and gloves if you wish, my lady," he said.

Abby stared at him in surprise. "I am not alone. My friends have accompanied me and will be along any moment."

Rather than open the door as she expected him to do, he stepped past her. "If you'll just follow me, my lady."

Abby didn't follow. Instead, she pulled open the door herself, only to gape at the empty street below. Prudence and Sophia had left her? What the devil was going on? Where was she?

She spun around to face the butler. "Tell me who employs you, sir."

"If you'll be good enough to give me your damp outer garments, I will take you to him."

How very cryptic. Abby looked at the man warily, finally concluding that if her friends had orchestrated this, there was nothing to fear. Ever so slowly, she removed her pelisse and gloves, then handed over her bonnet as well. A maid appeared, and the butler passed the garments to her.

Abby looked around, trying to find something familiar, but she was certain she'd never stood in this house before. Pristine white marble floors and stained wooden walls encased her. It was curiosity and curiosity alone that motivated her to follow the butler.

Her footsteps echoed in the hall, mingling with the eerie sound of pounding rain. The butler stopped next to an open door, gesturing for her to enter.

It was a ballroom.

She walked in slowly, cautiously, curiously—at least until she spied Brigston leaning casually against a wall not far from her, looking so handsome in a dark green waistcoat and tan breeches. He twirled a shuttlecock in one hand while two rackets lay at his feet.

Abby's pulse quickened. She looked from him to the rain-splattered windows beyond, recalling the day she last played shuttlecock with him at Oakley. In an instant, the house took on a wonderful air of familiarity.

She stared pointedly at the rackets at his feet. "You cannot be serious," she said.

"Oh, but I am." He pushed away from the wall and strolled towards her. As he did so, a giddy sensation spread through her stomach. She tried her best to keep her heart from hammering and her lips from twitching, but failed.

"I've already won and you lost, remember?" she said. "You really must learn to accept that and move on with your life."

"I fully intend to move on with it." He tossed the shuttlecock aside and threaded his fingers through hers, sending shivers of delight up and down her arms. "That is where you come in, my lady."

"Me?" She looked at him, imploringly, fearfully, battling against the hope that threatened to overwhelm her.

He pulled her closer. "I'm afraid you will not be able to hire Theo as your maid of all work after all."

"Why not?"

"Because you don't need a cottage, nor will you ever require one," he said.

"Why?" she asked again, probably sounding like a nincompoop. But try as she might, she couldn't think clearly. His touch paralyzed her, his eyes mesmerized her, and his mouth transfixed her. The familiar scent of his cologne only added to the headiness.

Kiss me before this beautiful dream disappears, she thought.

He kissed the knuckles on her hand instead. "Marry me, Abby."

Her body trembled, or perhaps it was the room. She couldn't tell. Was this truly happening? She didn't dare to believe it. "How can I? Nothing has changed."

"Everything has changed," he said. "I've realized I cannot live without you."

"But your title, your inheritance—"

"Will be secure, so long as we produce an heir."

"How?" she asked again, desperately wanting to understand.

He grinned wickedly. "How will we produce an heir?"

Her face flamed. "That is not what I meant and you know it. Now cease teasing me and tell me how I can possibly marry you. The Marriage Act is still in place, is it not?"

"In England, yes, but not in France. You need only accompany me to Paris and marry me there."

She blinked at him in awe. All this time, she'd seen

nothing but walls and barricades while Brigston had managed to uncover a door somewhere, or perhaps he'd just knocked a hole through the plaster.

"Is it really that simple?" she asked.

He shrugged. "I wouldn't say simple. It's a long journey to Paris, and when we return there will be talk. A lot of it. Our acceptance among the ton may suffer, your reputation in particular. To elope once was one thing. To elope a second time with a man England looks upon as your brother is another."

Abby didn't care about any of that. She wound her arms around his neck and snuggled close. "According to Prudence, a person's life would be dull indeed without a little scandal attached to their name."

"I've always considered Lady Knave to be wise." His arms circled her waist, and he dropped his forehead to hers. "Say you'll run away to Paris with me, Abby."

"Only if you kiss me," she answered.

He complied, and Abby was immediately taken back to that day in the woods when he'd kissed her before. Only this time, it wasn't just hope and possibilities that carried her afloat, it was the knowledge that she would finally be able to marry the man she loved, the only man she wanted to love. This was the start of something remarkable. Abby could feel it in her bones.

Brigston continued to kiss her, moving from her lips to her neck. Abby delighted in each and every sensation. *I was meant to be with this man,* she thought.

A loud clap of thunder shook the ballroom, and Abby pulled free with a gasp. She looked out the windows near the back of the ballroom, where she was sure she'd find evidence of a lighting strike, but all was well.

Brigston chuckled and gathered her close, holding her

tightly against him. "Apparently, my kiss can make the ground shake."

"I believe it was *my* kiss," Abby countered. With her head buried against his chest, she could hear his heart thump, feel his tightened chest against her cheek, and smell the citrus and spice she'd grown to love.

This was her home.

"I believe it was *I* who kissed *you*," he reminded her.

"Yes, but I told you to kiss me."

"Why should that matter?"

Abby opened her mouth to explain, but she couldn't think of any additional arguments, so she playfully threaded her fingers through his hair instead. Such soft hair. "Can we not think of it as *our* kiss?"

"No."

She laughed. "Then I'll have to become very brazen and be the one to kiss you during thunderstorms from this point forward. Not only will I make the ground shake, but I'll make a rainbow appear in the sky afterwards."

"I give you leave to try all you'd like." He grinned and dropped another kiss on her lips before scooping up the shuttlecock. "In the meantime. I believe I have a game of shuttlecock to win."

She pouted. "You really were in earnest."

"Did you doubt it?" He retrieved the rackets and held one out to her.

She didn't take it right away, arching an eyebrow instead. "Before we begin, you should know that this was my favorite childhood game, and I'm quite good at it."

"Quite good at inventing unreasonable rules, you mean," he quipped.

She took the racket from him and smiled. "I'm good at that, too. Very well. Let us see you try to best me, sir."

"I will do my utmost," he promised and tossed her the shuttlecock.

EPILOGUE

Four and One Half Months Later

WEDDING BELLS CHIMED as Abby exited the chapel hand in hand with her husband. No one awaited them, no friendly faces or fanfare of any sort, just a sunny, late-August morning in Paris. A few people passed by on the street below, but that didn't stop her husband from pulling her against him and kissing her soundly.

One man whistled, making Abby blush and Brigston laugh.

As soon as parliament had concluded six weeks prior, Abby and Anne returned to Oakley with Brigston and his mother, taking Theo along with them. Although they couldn't grant her the promised job of a maid of all work, Brigston had a better position in mind, a position that brought a smile to the girl's lips and an excited flush to her cheeks. She was now assisting Monsieur Roch in the kitchen. At the time, Abby could only pray Theo would learn quickly and not upset the French cook too much—she knew from experience he was not the most patient of men—but Theo had surprised them all. She'd worked hard, adapted quickly, and now Monsieur Roch couldn't do without her.

Brigston assisted Abby into the barouche, and she settled happily in, smoothing out the folds of her blue silk gown. There was a reason she'd asked Brigston if they could wait until August to marry. Abby was officially out of mourning and could wear whichever color she wished. For her wedding gown, she'd chosen Jasper's favorite—sky blue. Over a year ago, he'd begun a journey with her that had ultimately led her here, and while he may be gone, his memory would live on through her, through her husband, through their mother, and through Anne.

Thank you, Jasper, she thought as the barouche jolted forward, carrying them towards their first stop of their wedding trip—a grand hotel only a few blocks away. Over the next couple of weeks, they'd take in the sights of Paris, visit the surrounding countryside, and enjoy a few days in Calais before journeying back to Oakley.

Abby tilted her face to the sunshine and then to her husband. How wonderful that sounded.

My husband.

He brought her hand to his lips and placed a kiss on her palm. "I was hoping a thunderstorm would come through while we were in the church," he said. He always teased her about that, the toad.

"I'm beginning to think I must be the superior kisser if you are always hoping for thunderstorms," she said pertly.

He barked out a laugh. "Think what you wish, my lady. We both know the truth."

The coach turned, taking them down a cobblestone street with the Louvre on the right and the Seine on the left. The imposing dome of the Collège des Quatre-Nations could be seen in the distance. It was a striking sight, one that Abby had never imagined she'd see.

"Do you think little Anne is well?" she mused.

He snickered. "After three weeks of Mother's constant cosseting, there will be no living with her when we return."

Abby leaned her head against his shoulder and smiled. "Admit it. You could never live without her."

"I could live without ruined shirts and cravats and late night howlings that shake the house almost as much as my kisses."

Abby laughed, knowing he didn't mean a word of it. It had taken longer for him to warm up to little Anne than his mother, but the day she'd grabbed hold of his cravat, pulled the knot loose, and stuffed the fabric into her mouth had been the day he'd been smitten. Abby recognized the look in his eyes. Now he doted on her almost as thoroughly as their mother did.

"I was thinking," said Brigston, "that we could stop at a park for a quick game of shuttlecock before luncheon. What do you say?"

He was teasing her again, or so she hoped. Sometimes she wasn't entirely certain, but honestly, shuttlecock? Now? In her wedding gown? Would she never hear the end of that wretched game? She'd finally conceded that he was, and always would be, the reigning champion.

"I'd say that I never liked the game and have no wish to play it ever again."

He threw his head back and laughed, drawing the attention of several passersby. "The truth has finally come out, I see. I was wondering how much more teasing you'd endure before I wore you down."

"Isn't this a wonderful start to our marriage," she said dryly.

"What did you expect when we thwarted the law by fleeing England to marry? Frankly, I see only bad luck in our future."

"How morose of you to say such things. Never say I've married a cynic."

"I'm afraid you have, my love, but perhaps you can reform me. You did say your kisses can bring about rainbows."

The man was incorrigible, and his sense of humor infectious. Abby fought her twitching lips before succumbing to a giggle. "How right you are," she said and kissed his cheek.

His brow furrowed a moment before he shook his head. "I don't see a rainbow. You'd best try again."

"Wretch." She tucked her arm through his, snuggled closer, and let the barouche carry them away. Only a year ago, she'd been an expectant widow with no means, no real family to speak of, and a bleak-looking future before her. Now she was a wife, mother, and daughter.

She used to believe she was wrong to hope, that it would always let her down. How silly of her to think that. Hope was not to blame. Life was. Disappointment came to all no matter their situation. Sometimes it tripped, sometimes it shoved, and sometimes it ran roughshod over a person. What mattered was not how one fell, but whether or not he or she chose to rise again—or in Abby's experience, *hope* again.

And she would. Always.

Dear Reader,

Thanks so much for reading! I hope this story gave you a break from the daily grind and rejuvenated you in some way. This is the second installment of my new Serendipity series. If you'd like to be notified when Sophia's story becomes available (or any future release), you can sign up for my New Release List at RachaelReneeAnderson.com or follow me on Amazon.

If you can spare a few minutes, I'd be incredibly grateful for a review from you on Goodreads or Amazon. Even though I can't thank you personally, I am always so grateful when readers take a few minutes to review a book.

May your days be filled with beauty and happiness!

Rachael

Coming next in the Serendipity Series . . .
The Solicitor's Son

ACKNOWLEDGEMENTS

As always, thank you, MOM and LETHA, for brainstorming with me, listening to my ramblings, and helping me to plot out my stories. You have both been a huge blessing in all aspects of my life.

MEGAN JACOBSON, bless you for sharing your historical knowledge with me. You helped me so much with both plotting this story and fine-tuning it in the end. I'm not sure what I would have done without you.

ALISON BLACKBURN, thank you for our daily walks and being so willing to talk books with me. You also happen to be a awesome content editor! How did I get so lucky?

ANDREA PEARSON, so grateful for your friendship, as always. Thanks for always reading my stuff and pointing out both the positives and the problems. You're the best!

KAREY WHITE, bless you for only being a phone call or text message away, for helping me come up with this series title, and for sharing your brilliant editing skills with me. I don't even want to contemplate what I'd do without your help.

KATHY HABEL, many MANY thanks for your friendship and help with anything and everything involving marketing. That's my least favorite aspect of this business, and I will be forever grateful for your many skills in that area.

JEFF, BRIGHTON, KENNEDY, DEVON, AND TAYCEE, you're the best. And I mean THE BEST.

I'm especially grateful to my Heavenly Father, for challenging, inspiring, and blessing me.

LOVE YOU ALL!!!

ABOUT RACHAEL ANDERSON

RACHAEL ANDERSON is a *USA Today* bestselling author and mother of four crazy but awesome kids. Over the years she's gotten pretty good at breaking up fights or at least sending guilty parties to their rooms. She can't sing, doesn't dance, and despises tragedies, but she recently figured out how yeast works and can now make homemade bread, which she is really good at eating. You can read more about her and her books online at RachaelReneeAnderson.com.

Made in the USA
Columbia, SC
07 December 2018